# BET IT *Run*

## THE RUN AND HIDE DUET

## ALINA MAY

*To all my dirty, nasty hoes: you ready to have some fun?*

# AUTHOR'S NOTE

To all my dark romance loving girlies: here is your trigger warning shoutout. If you're anything like me, you decide if you want the book based on your favorite TW's. That said: this is a dark romance. We love consent (outside of book worlds), so please, educate yourself first! This is a true I'd-like-to-kill-you enemies to (Stockholm) lovers. 'Lovers' is used loosely as there is no sappy romance in this book. In addition, although the main character is aroused for much of the book, almost the whole book contains non con. Please check my website for a full list of the trigger warnings (they're extensive). You can find me at alina-may-books.squarespace.com

The triggers found on my website can be coping mechanisms, exploration, or a way to relive the past in a safe environment. These things are not safe, sexy, or sane in the real world without consent and some of them are impossible to get consent for! If you do not like dub con and non con, DO NOT READ THIS BOOK. Stop here. Your mental well-being is far more important than reading this story.

here. Your mental well-being is far more important than reading this story.

If you're still here, boy do I have a fun ride for you. Sit back and enjoy. Take your power back girlies.

Love ya,
Alina

# Mary Jo

## 1

I HANG MY KEYS FROM THE BOOB-SHAPED HANGAR, HOLDING all my groceries in one hand. The store was packed with people who walked with no purpose, and I managed to get behind every single one of them.

Kyle sits on the couch, playing Xbox and barking orders into the headset. As I walk past him into the kitchen, he flips his phone over so I can't see the screen. A flash of irritation runs through me as I duck under the hanging vines that are taking over my kitchen and drop the groceries on the small island.

"Babe. I got food." I try to keep the sudden venom out of my tone.

He doesn't reply. I glare for a second, then pop in a microwave meal. The same sage chicken I've been hooked on for the past month. I start putting away the groceries as the food warms and smells pleasant. I pull open the freezer to put more meals away and shake my head. It's ironic that I review food for a living, but my most recent fixation has been a frozen meal from Walmart.

"God, are you eating that again?"

I snap my gaze up to him. He's still looking at the TV. He's dusty blond, toned, and has always dressed nicely, keeping up with the latest trends.

"You play the same game over and over, and you don't get tired of it." I roll my eyes. His phone chimes. I glare and add, "Plus, you can't tell me what to eat."

He doesn't flip his phone over to look at it.

It's nothing. Probably just an email. I stand to eat and open my phone. I had a video go viral about a year ago, and now I've built up a small platform to pay the bills and even do a few nice things, like pay off my car. We used to rely on Kyle's less-than-impressive income as a night shift security guard, and at that time, Ramen was my staple. That's what I started posting videos about—all the cheap, yummy ways I made Ramen interesting. And things took off from there.

I look at my phone and see I got fewer views on the video I posted this morning, as has been the trend recently. I turn it off again and look toward the living room. Kyle and I have been dating for a while. Started off like firecrackers, but recently, things have been slowing down. We haven't had sex in weeks, and before that, it was a month. Kyle says he's tired from work, although it never stopped him before. Coincidentally I've been a bit of a bitch recently.

Maybe that's why my views are down.

I finish my dinner and toss the empty container in the trash. I flip between chores and scrolling social media, picking up the clothes that Kyle throws next to the hamper and doing both our dishes. He likes the 'let it soak' method. I like the 'no bugs' method. As I work, I tell myself I'm overreacting. As I go, I methodically undress and casually walk between Kyle and the TV with no shirt, pants, or bra.

He finally looks up at me. "Nice." Then he goes back to telling Tucker to get behind cover.

The fucker.

I flop down on my bed and glare at the ceiling. A fight would be fun, but it never gets anywhere with him. It's getting boring to even pick them anymore as he predictably spins the blame around on me and then leaves the house in a muted huff. It's fine. I'll take care of myself. I slide my hand down to my thong. I rub tight but light circles around my clit, trying to clear my mind. I think about the gorgeous blond woman I watched get dominated by her partner in my porn browsing last night. They are my favorites. He makes noise, and she isn't putting on a show. He spanks, bites, chokes her, and she always fights back until she comes. I tried showing it to Kyle once. He looked disgusted and asked why I liked domestic violence.

I rub harder circles around my clit, feeling the blood rush to my pussy. I keep at it until I come. It isn't hard or electrifying, but it gets the job done. I don't go for a second orgasm. I just turn on some ASMR and pull the blankets over my shoulders. At some point, Kyle turns off the TV and bumps around, eventually leaving the house for work, and I fall into a fitful sleep.

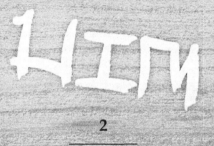

## 2

I GLARE AT MY PHONE. SHE'S SO PRETTY WHEN SHE SLEEPS, her blond hair fanned out, her arms splayed, her body open and vulnerable to attack. Her features are delicate, and her body is petite, only adding to her helplessness. I curl my lip in disgust.

I shift in my seat, parked a block away from her house. It's a run-down, middle to lower-class neighborhood, so no one asks why I've been sitting in my running car for hours. I used a different rental car this time, just in case anyone was paying attention. I check the footage from the small camera I put on her dresser, facing her bed. I had watched her half-ass masturbation session earlier. It made my dick hard.

Which made me angry.

I turn my lights on and drive off, driving past her house, my headlights briefly lighting up her bedroom window. I keep going.

*Soon, kitten.* Very soon.

# Mary Jo

## 3

A FEW EVENINGS LATER, I SIT ON VIDEO CHAT WITH CARISSA, wine-drunk on the couch, and talk about our next vacation spot for the hundredth time.

"Bitch, I'm telling you, Mexico is next. Forget Florida." Her voice slurs a little.

"I'm so down," I laugh. We've visited every state between Ohio and Texas, where she is, and she's always ready to chase that next spot with me. As I put my empty wine glass on the coffee table, a tingly feeling rolled down my back. I shiver. This damn house and its drafts.

"Maybe we can find you a hot woman down there."

I looked back down at the brunette woman on my screen. "Kyle flipped out last time, remember? He said girls kissing is hot, but when I kissed a girl on New Year's, he cried for two hours." I was no longer seeing two of her, but the alcohol still warmed me pleasantly.

"Yeah, well, Kyle's a fucking weirdo."

I grunt, wrapping my fleece blanket around me for another chill. We talk for a while longer, and then I sign off, exhausted. Since Kyle is at work again, I turn off the lights. My bedroom is right off the kitchen, and I turn that light off last and drop into bed. I scroll online mindlessly, and at some point, pass out.

~

A HEAVY WEIGHT clamps over my mouth, and I startle awake. I blink in the dark, trying to figure out why it's hard to breathe. There's a weight on my chest. No, not a weight. A person.

I scream. It's muffled by the weight on my mouth.

A low, unfamiliar voice chuckles in my ear. "Easy, kitten. Relax, and this will go easier for you."

My heart rate begins to pound. What's going on? Who is this? I kick and make contact with something.

His weight continues to press into me, even heavier. I kick harder while trying to thrash and try to get my hands up. I'm crushed under him, but I get one hand up and immediately try to plunge my fingers into where I think the asshole's eyes should be. I get a chuckle and a hard knock to the side of my head that stalls me for a second.

"Or you can fight. I like it better that way." His voice is low and unconcerned. The weight is removed from my face for a second, and something burns in my neck. I scream again, thrashing and throwing my head up toward the man's shadowed head.

I make contact. Something warm and sticky drops into my eyes and over my cheeks, and he shifts on me. My right hand is semi-free, and I rake my fingernails up to his head and make contact with his clothes. I try again and feel my head begin to spin. Am I still drunk? I rake my fingers down again and get a grunt of pain followed by a growl of a laugh in my left ear.

"Get off me, bastard. I'm gonna kill you."

"Now, now, kitten. It's not nice to threaten people."

Rage surges through my blood, hot and heavy. The spinning gets more violent. I swing my right hand again, beating down on where I guess his ribs to be. My arm starts to move slower and lighter despite my maximum efforts to pound him into the wall next to my bed. It feels like I'm in a bad dream.

"Relax. Let it do its thing."

"Let what do its thing...prick...bastard." My tongue feels heavy in my mouth. I keep swinging, only to realize my hand is barely moving. The dark shadows above me swim. I taste blood.

"Good girl."

I growl out an insult, but it doesn't come out as comfortable warmth surrounds me. I get cocooned in relaxation. I pop my head up to get away, but it sucks me back under, and darkness envelops me.

PAIN SEARS THROUGH MY SKULL. My mind spins, and my throat is raw. I clench my eyes shut, not ready to let in any light.

Holy shit, I really outdid myself on the drinking. I'm going to have to tell Carissa to cut me off next time.

I blink open my eyes. I'm lying down, and there's a wooden wall in front of me. I blink a few times. I don't recognize where I am. What the—?

My gaze darts to the right side of the room. I'm on a small bed in a small...bedroom? Light pours in from behind me, and I crane my neck to see a small window with blinds pulled closed.

Something shifts on my left. I jerk my head around and see a man relaxed in a chair, watching me. He's big and muscled with dark tattoos down both arms. He appears in his early thirties with dark hair and light stubble on his jawline. His dark eyes flash.

"Hello, Mary." His voice is gravel.

I jerk upright, causing the spinning to start again.

"I'm not—who are you?"

"Your given name—Mary. Mary Jo Hall. You hate it, so you go by your middle name."

I squint. "How did you know—who are you?"

He shrugs. "Prick bastard, according to you."

That flashes a memory in my mind. Struggling. Pain. It all rushes back, and a surge of rage fills me.

"You mother—" I jerk forward, seeing my hands wrap around his throat in my mind. My body abruptly stops with my ass on the edge of the bed. Sharp pain jerks my right hand to a halt. I look down. I'm cuffed to a short chain that is wrapped around the bedpost.

"Yeah, sorry about that. My eyes are pretty, and I wanted to keep them." The man stands and leans in with a sneer. "Mary Jo, 29 years old. Makes videos reviewing food and became popular by creating meals under five dollars. Just paid off your Honda Civic, used to work at a few factories, and are now an influencer. A mom and dad who are still together, no siblings, best friend Carissa, and a boyfriend who works for Knight Security. Your favorite color is blue, you masturbate every night because your deadbeat boyfriend won't get it up for you, and you have no pets because he won't let you." His dark eyes stare into mine.

I simply stare at him. He has long dark eyelashes that contrast with an otherwise hard and masculine face. I have no idea how he knows all that. Fear tries to break through the anger. My heart flutters, and I pull in a breath.

He must see the shift. He smiles deeply. It doesn't reach his eyes.

"Good. Now, there are a few rules. One. If you try to attack me again, I'll hurt you. Two. I won't hurt you if you listen to my rules. So listen to my rules." He leans closer, and instinct tells me to back up. I glare at him instead. He's inches from my face.

"Three. If you run, I'll punish you." His breath brushes my face and smells of mint. "We're miles into the hills with no cell service and no neighbors except for black bears and coyotes."

Miles into the hills? How far from home did he take me? We

only had cornfields and beans where I was from. So many questions bounce in my brain.

He waits, watching my eyes.

I focus on him and narrow my eyes in return.

"So...no Doordash?"

Something flickers in his expression, and then he returns to his blank stare.

I should be afraid. Fear is battering my anger, trying to take over. I don't let it. Not right now. Not in front of him.

He steps back and straightens. He's a tall motherfucker, at least 6'2". And built. He could easily fold me in half and break me.

"Think about the rules, Mary." He walks to the door on the right side of the small room.

"Hey–"

He walks out and slams the door.

I sit stunned for a second. Then I scramble up on the bed again and examine my right hand, which is shackled to the frame. The metal cuff is snug against my wrist but not enough to pinch. The other end is secured to a thick chain, which is padlocked firmly to the bed frame. I have about a foot of slack. I hop off the bed and see the metal frame bolted to the floor.

What the hell?

I look around again. Near me is an empty plastic bucket and two bottles of water. The rest of the room is empty, except for the chair he was sitting in. No nightstands, no lamps. Just the door and the bed. I turn to the window and look out the blinds. It's daytime. The sun is shining on a small clearing, maybe fifty feet from the window, and then woods. I crane to see to the left and right. Just out of view to my right is what looks like a shed or garage. To the left is a dirt driveway that extends into the woods. With limited movement from my right hand, I feel around the window as best I can. It's small but big enough for me to crawl out of. The latch opens, but when I try to push it open, it doesn't budge. I look around more and see it's been nailed shut.

Fuck.

I turn back around. What the hell is going on? Is he going to rape me? Why did he keep calling me Mary? I don't know this man from Adam. I'd definitely remember him. Did I piss somebody off recently?

I stare at the door and think back to my recent videos. None were controversial. I got the normal hate comments, but my moderators take care of most of them before I see them. Fuck. Had this man been one of those commenters that who blocked and removed before I saw it? Also, how did he know so many things about me? I fiercely guard my personal information online.

I rub my face. Little dark flecks fall into my hand. Blood. His blood from the struggle.

Holy shit, he knew about me masturbating. What the actual hell?

My heart races.

He was in my home. While I slept. Is Kyle okay?

I look down at my clothes. I'm wearing the same leggings and pink tank top I fell asleep in. I have no shoes or socks. With massive relief, I realize I don't feel sore anywhere but my head. Not that that means I'm safe.

I sit on the edge of the bed.

What the fuck does he want me for?

I don't have money. My parents sure as fuck don't have money.

The longer I sit and think, the more worried I get. I don't like the reasons I could be here. He said he won't hurt me, but I don't believe him for a second. He was trying to get me to be compliant. So I would...do what?

I sit and stare at the wooden wall opposite the bed. I stare and stare. Shadows move across my lap. The room is silent. I hear the heat kick on every now and again. I count the headache pulses in my head rhythmically. The counting drowns out the questions.

The room begins to grow dark. I snap out of my stare-down with the wall, and my heart kicks up again. There are still no sounds outside the door. I glance at the water and the bucket. There's no bathroom.

That arrogant fucker expects me to piss in the bucket.

Rage fills me again. I won't do it. I'll piss all over his floor before I piss in that damn bucket.

The room gets fully dark before I grab a water. I examine it all over, looking for tamper marks. It's fully sealed, and nothing comes out when I squeeze. Reluctantly, I open it and take a sip. Instantly, it cools my mouth and fills me with thirst. I suck it down, not realizing how thirsty I was. I'm going to make it out of this, I decide. I'm going to play whatever game I have to in order to win this.

I wait all night for him to come back in. I fall into fitful sleep sitting straight up, my empty water bottle in my hand like a weapon.

He never does.

# HIM

## 4

THE PLAN WENT OFF WITH BARELY A HITCH. I BRING A GLASS of bourbon to my lips and relish the burn as it goes down. I sit on the couch, knowing she won't get anywhere tonight. I made sure she was secure after I went through all that work to get her here.

My nose still hurts from where she bashed it. It pissed me off when she did it, but it also made me rock hard. The way she fought me... made me want to sink into her heat. To take what she didn't want to give. Watching her soft, unconscious form earlier was intoxicating in an infuriating way. I had to leave the room. I wanted to hurt her. Wanted to mark that pretty pale skin.

She must have looked like a drunk college kid when I carried her to the car. At least, that's what I'm hoping. I smirk as I think about how I staged her breakup note with my pictures. The fact that her boyfriend was cheating on her was the icing on the cake. It made her strongly worded breakup note credible. I couldn't have created a better situation myself. I took her clothes and makeup and other bullshit and wrote 'fuck you' all over the walls in lipstick. That was a risk because of the handwriting, but Kyle only cared about saving face. I told him she didn't want him to contact her again, or she'd call the cops.

My blood on her sheets was an unexpected hurdle and cost me some time as I had to take those and search her closets to remake her bed.

I glance over my drink. She's so naive. Didn't expect anything bad to ever happen to her. Didn't expect to have to protect her things and phone from people like me. I used her face to unlock her phone and posted a short video on her page with text that she had found an exciting business opportunity, but she couldn't say much because the company asked her to keep it a secret, and she was really busy. I'm proud that I put some inspirational music behind it and even a few of her favorite stickers.

It will buy me a few days before someone reports her missing. When they do, it'll take at least two more days to get any kind of search. Cops don't take missing adults seriously unless they're addicts, mentally ill, or there's evidence of foul play. Which there isn't. I made sure of that. And when they do look, there are no links to me. I turned her phone off, took the SIM card out of it, and dropped it in her backyard.

I take another burning sip and smile to myself.

She is mine now. And I'll make her pay.

# Mary Jo

## 5

I jerk awake. The morning light seeps in through the window. Shit, I must have fallen asleep. My neck is stiff from letting it hang.

I hear a sound by the door. I stiffen and sit up.

The door opens, and *he* comes in, looking at the bucket, one bottle of water, and then me. We are both silent for a minute, each measuring the other up. He's in blue jeans today and a black T. It stretches across his chest. Tattoos crawl over both arms.

He walks over to me and goes for my right hand. I back up.

"Give me your hand." He holds out his impatiently.

I look at the ink that swirls around his wrist.

Every atom wants me to tell him to go fuck himself. But I don't. I give my hand over like an obedient puppy.

He fishes a key out of his pocket and unlocks my wrist cuff. I rub the sore skin and flex in freedom.

"Come."

He turns and walks out of the room.

I jump off the bed and follow. My joints ache in protest, and my bladder twinges against the movement.

The man waits in the hallway. Behind him, the space opens

into what appears to be a dining room on the right and a kitchen further on. The wood paneling continues. Almost like we're in a cabin.

He jerks his head towards a door on my right.

"Bathroom."

Hope sparks in me, and I enter the small bathroom with another small window. There is just a toilet and a sink with a mirror above it. I move to shut the door, and he jams his foot in.

"Are you kidding?" I can't help the anger that laces my tone.

He just cocks an eyebrow.

I cross my arms. "I need to pee. Get out of the way."

"No."

I growl, "Yes. I won't try to escape. I just need to pee. I can't pee if someone is watching."

He crosses his arms and stands there.

Fuck. I'm trying to be meek, but my bladder painfully locks up at the thought of him watching. I cross my legs and jiggle a little. I go back and forth with myself briefly. My cheeks burn as I consider peeing in front of this dangerous man who is staring at me intently. My bladder hurts. Finally, I pull my pants down as little as possible and try to angle my body away from him. I glare at where the floor meets the wall.

I wait.

After what feels like an eternity, he shifts. "What are you doing?"

Not peeing. I internally roll my eyes but keep my voice low. "I told you I can't pee if someone is watching."

"There's always the bucket."

"No. Let me just..." I reach over to the sink and turn the water on. I glance at him, and he's staring at me. I try again. Finally, the pain in my bladder wins out, and I pee. My face flames.

I wash my hands and splash a little in my mouth. My breath is horrible, and I stink.

He steps out of the doorway and walks towards the kitchen. "Come."

I glare at his back. I'm not his damn dog. But I follow.

On my right is a dining room, along with what appears to be the front door. On my immediate left is a spiral staircase. The living room has high ceilings. Big windows open up to the wintery yard with trees beyond. There is comfortable furniture and a fireplace. The place is covered with red and black moose and bear decor.

The man is in the kitchen, pulling out bread and peanut butter.

"Windows and doors are secured, so don't try."

I stand at the kitchen island. There is virtually nothing on the counters. The knife he's using to spread the peanut butter is plastic.

"Do you want money?"

He remains quiet.

"Did you find me online?" Stalk me? Beat his meat to me thinking he could have me? My stomach sinks.

"Eat." He hands me a sandwich and sucks some peanut butter off his finger. I watch his mouth close around the finger, lips pulling on it. I shake my head in anger. He's pretty but so cold. Evil.

He smirks.

I devour the sandwich as he makes another. I eat that one as well.

A jarring ringing fills the silence, and I jump. He pulls a blocky-looking phone out of his pocket. He glares at it, then at me.

"Remember the rules." He steps to the front door and answers it just before stepping outside and slamming the door. A small chime of an alarm goes off when the door is opened.

I stand dumbfounded. I look around the cabin. I hear his low voice just outside the door. My first instinct is to run. I want to break out the back windows and go. I start that way, then pause.

This is a test; I know it is. He could have chained me back up and then taken the call, but he's trying to see if I'll obey.

I don't want to. I want to scream and punch and run. I clench my fists, my body shaking with the fight to redirect my adrenaline. It pisses me off, but he has the upper hand right now. It won't do me any good to show my cards when he's expecting me to.

I bite my tongue and look around the living room for anything that could help me. I look up. There's an open loft with a wooden railing. I check the windows in the living room. They're also nailed closed.

I move back to the kitchen and slowly open a cabinet. It doesn't squeak. Inside, I find paper plates and bowls. I open cabinet after cabinet and drawer after drawer. Trying to get anything—a toothpick, a fork, a bill with his name on it. They're virtually empty. Like he removed everything, knowing I'd go through them.

His deep voice continues outside. It sounds like he's arguing with someone.

I open the fridge. There are three cartons of eggs, milk, cheese, a bunch of chicken thighs, and barbecue sauce...enough to feed a few people for at least a week. In the freezer are a bunch of frozen meals, neatly arranged. Dread sinks in my stomach when I see a familiar stack of my sage chicken meals. How does he know? He has been stalking me. Fear runs currents around my bones. But don't I have to have some sign that he's been stalking me for that to apply? Some declaration of love? He seems repulsed by me. Confusion fills me. But I guess the meals mean he probably plans on keeping me alive for at least a little. I counted seven of them.

My stomach hurts.

I move to the bathroom. I could break the mirror if I needed to. That's the only useful thing in there. There's a door across from the bathroom, and I open it. From what I can see, wooden steps go down in a half staircase into what must be a basement.

A hard hand grabs where my shoulder meets my neck. I squeak.

"Trying to run, little kitten?"

"No." I hate myself for showing him a little fear. How in the world was he so damn quiet? I turn around to face him. He waits, maybe expecting me to give a smart-ass response, but I bite my tongue and picture punching him right in his pretty face.

It makes me smile.

He seems disappointed and shoves me back to my room with a bored look. He locks me up again and leaves me once more.

FOR THE NEXT FEW HOURS, I try to formulate a plan. The man doesn't ask me for anything, so maybe he's been paid to give me to someone else. I won't give him that opportunity. I drink as much water as I can, use the restroom when he lets me, and eat the sandwich dinner he provides. I ask for another, and he gives it to me.

I try to sedate him into complacency. Which is pretty fucking hard to do when he doesn't ask for anything. It's like we're stuck in a stalemate. The tension is thick in the air. Once, he caught me rolling my eyes at him, and his smirk was deadly.

I'm not sure what rules he isn't telling me, but I know they're there, and it feels inevitable that I'll break one. Well, I know I'll break one when I kill him, and it'll feel fucking amazing. I've stayed angry. I don't let myself feel anything else.

Slowly, he gives me more freedom. After the first day, he lets me use the bathroom alone and gives me a stick of deodorant and a stack of my clothes, which I presume he got from my room. Which is awfully invasive of him.

The next day, he lets me fix my own sandwiches while he makes eggs. I spend most of my time trying to get the wire out of my bra to pick the lock with, but it's sewn in so tight. I steal a plastic knife and saw the material. It takes a while, but the wire pops out. Only it's too thick to pick the handcuffs with, which leaves me with a ruined bra and no alternatives.

I try not to think about Kyle and Carissa. They'll know I'm gone. What are they thinking happened to me? How long until they go through my social media and find him? How long until they find me? The thought makes me sad.

On the third day, he doesn't chain me to my bed.

In the afternoon, we both sit in the living room. I hit him with my usual barrage of questions in the morning, going from angry to frantic, back to angry. We've been silent for hours. Finally, I break my silence, "Who were you talking to outside the other day? On the phone?"

He's working on some small engine that he brought in from outside. He looks up at me like he forgot I was there.

"A friend."

Real descriptive, this fucker. I scratch my scalp under my greasy hair. I've tried to wash it in the sink, but one can only get so far.

"What is that for?" I stand behind him.

He grunts, "ATV." He works for a few more minutes in silence. Then something clings so loud it makes me jump.

"Fuck." He drops the wrench he was using and brings his left hand to his mouth.

I look from him to the wrench. Adrenaline fills my body, and I don't think, just act. I rush to grab it. He moves to stop me, but he's not fast enough. I swing it around, aiming for his head. I make contact, slamming into his skull.

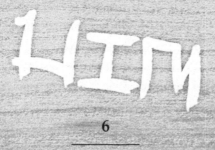

# HIM

## 6

I'M ALREADY MOVING WHEN THE WRENCH CRASHES INTO ME, and I'm stunned. Pain slams into me, and I close my eyes. I open them again, and I'm lying on the ground. She's over me, swinging again.

I roll towards her, closing the distance between us. Her strike falls against my back. I wrap my arms around her middle and yank her to the ground. She screams and curls onto her side, and rolls out from under me. I follow, crawling over her, breathing heavily.

I saw it in her eyes. She was going to try and kill me.

I laugh despite the pain. A hint of respect curls up inside me.

Under me, she screams and swipes at my face, scratching down my cheek. That scream...damn near makes me shiver in pleasure. I drop my weight on her and pin her left arm to the floor by her head with both of mine. She tries to straighten it, but I pull her into a shoulder lock and apply pressure.

"Stop."

Her back bows with the pain I'm sending down her arm. She keeps fighting.

I pull down on her arm a little harder. "Stop. I'll break it if you don't."

That gets her attention. She stills beneath me, panting. I look into her pretty blue eyes. They are wild and full of hatred and fear. I eat up that delicious emotion like a starving man to a feast. It makes me feel heady despite the pain from her hit. I take a deep breath of her.

"Are you...hard?" she grits out and pauses, evaluating. Fiery emotion fills her eyes. "I—you sick motherfucker. Let me go, you goddamned animal. I'm going to rip your balls from your body with my fingernails and shove them so far up your asshole that you won't see them for another two weeks. I—" She stops when I begin chuckling. Rage lights in her eyes, making them so bright they sparkle. It's been so fun watching her feel me out and tamp down her hatred and glorious fear. Waiting to see what she'd do, which rule she'd break first, and now she's broken one.

What a violent kitten. I can't help myself; I love it.

She's still heaving for breath under me. Her fear is not misplaced. I won't lie.

"A or B?"

"What?"

I cock an eyebrow. "A? Or B?"

"Neither, you cocksucker."

"Tsk, the mouth on you. If you don't pick, you'll get both."

She pinches her lips together, debating if I'm lying.

"B."

"Good girl." I release her, getting up quickly and pulling her up by her neck. I escort her back to her room and cuff her back to the bed. Then I leave the room and shut the door.

# Mary Jo

## 7

I TREMBLE ON THE BED. I FAILED, AND NOW HE WAS MORE alive than I'd seen him in the past three days, his gaze on fire. He is going to kill me. I had my big chance, and now, whatever game we were playing is over.

I jump when he comes back through the door. He's holding a wooden board. No, a paddle. With some sort of cutout in it. He unlocks my cuff, and I immediately dart towards the door. He snatches me up by the hair and yanks hard so I fall with my upper body on the bed.

"Fuck you." A tear leaks down my face from the sharp pain on my scalp. He doesn't let up. I fight anyway. "Let me go!"

"I told you the rules. This is on you, kitten."

I fight harder, desperation filling me. He holds me down easily. He puts his head by my ear and takes a deep breath. He then yanks my pants down.

Oh fuck. I had resolved myself to death, but not rape. Real panic takes over for the first time since waking up here despite my struggle to keep it down. I kick and scratch and hit.

"Three hits for attacking me, kitten."

Thwack. A sharp pain explodes across my ass and then blossoms into burning. I lay there stunned. It hurts deeply. Then there's something, a hand, massaging the spot.

"There you go. If you want to act like a bad girl, you'll have to take it like a bad girl."

Did he just...spank me?

Thwack. It comes again, and I wasn't ready. It hurts more than the last time. Despite myself, I let out a small sound of pain and start fighting again.

His hand returns, massaging the burning pain, his other hand still deeply rooted in my hair.

"Push your ass up, and I'll think you like it, dirty girl."

"Stop! Let me g—"

THWACK. I screech, the pain becoming a haze in my mind. The hand is back again, massaging buzzing tingles of pleasure through my ass.

"You sound so good screaming for me."

More tears leak from my eyes, and I hate myself for it. I tell myself it's because of the sharp hold on my hair.

"All done. You fight me again, and it'll be five." He releases my hair and leans in. I turn my face away from him. Shame burns through me, as does something else. Something...fiercer.

With horror, I realize I'm pressing my thighs together. I stop. What the fuck is wrong with me?

The man gathers the paddle and re-chains me to the bed.

I stare at him, trying to tuck all that fear back in. "What's your name?"

He looks at me, and I'm suddenly aware of my puffy eyes. I look away, feeling calming anger start to creep in again.

"You can call me Sir."

Like fuck I will. I don't say anything.

He smiles. "You're going to be fun to break."

～

I DON'T SLEEP. It's been dark for a few hours. Shame and embarrassment keep filling my head. I push them out.

He didn't kill me. He has some sick perversion for hurting women. I'm almost more afraid now than I was before. I think back to all the times he's had a chance to hurt me and hasn't. This is some kind of game to him. I've heard of Doms asking their Subs to call them sir before. But that was always consensual.

My ass burns, and I have to shift to keep my weight off of it. He only hit the right side, making laying on my left side difficult with the little slack I have with the cuff. I imagine him sleeping peacefully, not bothered at all that I'm in pain and a prisoner.

That goddamned piece of shit.

The anger is back. I want him to pay. All the rules say are no running and no hurting him. He's stuck to his promises so far. He hasn't done anything until I break a rule, and instead of getting angry, he gets off when I do. So, I need to figure out how to break his cool demeanor without breaking a rule. Angry people make mistakes, but they also hurt people. But what's to say he isn't going to break his stupid rules and hurt me anyway?

I take my chain and hit it to the bedpost. It gives a delicious clank in the quiet. I throw myself into hitting it over and over. Clank. Clank. Clank. Clank.

I hit for what feels like thirty minutes, but it could be shorter or longer. I have no way of knowing for sure. I go through the full range of emotions as I do. Sometimes, I think about yelling an apology and never making another sound. Sometimes, I imagine his fingers in between the cuff and the metal post, and I hit harder. My arm is tired, and my fingers hurt from the constant small impacts.

"That's enough, kitten." His voice demands from right outside my door. I jump. I hadn't heard him approach.

The silence is loud. All I hear is the static in my head.

I wait for a while. Longer than I think it should take for him to walk back to bed. And then I wait some more.

*Clank. Clank. Clank.*

My door bursts open.

He stands there, looking tall and angry. The shadow is deeper on his face. His jaw ticks as he looks at me.

I smile sweetly.

In the blink of an eye, he's by my bed, uncuffing me and tossing me over his shoulder. I beat on his back, looking down at his ass and the floor as he marches me out.

"Let me go, you ogre! You ugly-ass, unwashed shaft of a—"

He marches me up the spiral staircase, and I bounce, the breath getting pushed out of my lungs.

He tosses me through the air, and I land on a king-sized bed. We're in the loft. I try to catch my breath. I scramble to get up, and he cocks an eyebrow. "Get up, and I'll spank your ass raw."

I pause.

He looks deadly serious.

"Since you can't behave on your own, you're going to sleep here with me, and you're going to be a good girl and keep quiet till morning."

I open my mouth, and he shoots me another look.

"Lay down, Mary."

I sit, frozen, eyeing his massive body. My mouth goes dry. What was he going to do to me?

"I'm not getting undressed."

He lays on the right side of the bed, the mattress dipping with his weight. "I didn't tell you to."

I sit rigid for a few minutes. This is far more dangerous than being downstairs.

He looks at me with demand in his eyes. "Lay. Down." He hasn't moved from his side of the bed.

I scoot as far from him as possible and lay on my back on the blankets. I refuse to look at him. My right asscheek smarts as I lay on it.

There's nothing but quiet breathing from his side. He's so close. I want to kill him. To smother him in his sleep.

I lay for as long as I could stand it, stiff and hurting. Finally, I'm forced to roll to my left side to face him. The relief is sweet.

I glare at his profile. He's lying on his back, arms above the covers, eyes closed. His dark lashes are stark against his skin. An angry red scratch flares down his cheek from our fight earlier. He breathes evenly and deeply. It smells masculine up here. A hint of musk and oil.

"Sleep, Mary."

I jump.

"My name isn't Mary," I grumble. But it is. And it scares me that he knows that. Did he talk to my parents? Did he hurt them?

Thoughts bounce in my head all night. I can't tell if he's asleep, and I don't want to risk him beating my ass because he would. I lay awake until the sunlight creeps into the loft, and I allow myself a moment. Emotions go rolling through me. Fear, loneliness, sadness, vulnerability. I let a single tear roll down my cheek and then lock it all up again.

THE MAN ACTS like nothing happened the next morning. He allows me to roam the house. I choose to sit on one of the couches and stare into the fireplace. I think about Kyle. I miss his hugs when he'd rest his chin on the top of my head. That brings a shot of pain in my heart, and I tamp it down, trying to think about anything but my home. As hard as I try, my thoughts keep going back.

There's a stack of books by the fireplace. It looks like some kind of cowboy romance.

He has been puttering around. He grabs one of the books, puts it on the couch next to me, and then goes down into the basement.

I perk up. This is the first time he's broken his line of sight with me without chaining me up.

I stand. Then I hesitate, frozen.

The sound of a key turning in a knob breaks me from my thoughts.

A key in the front door.

I turn to stare as the door opens, and a man steps in. The alarm softly chimes.

I feel like everything moves in slow motion. A man steps into the cabin. He's in his late twenties, with short blond hair, scruff, and an earring in his left ear. He's six feet, and it's obvious he's built as fuck under his hoodie.

He makes eye contact with me and stops. I see the surprise in his light eyes.

I rush for him. "Help, please help." I fist his hoodie, muttering gibberish. "A man took me. My name is Jo Hall, and I've been kidnapped. Please, let's go! We have to get away." I start tugging him towards the door.

He doesn't come with me.

"Please, I—" I plead and go to grab his arm again, but something in his eyes makes my blood run cold. He's smirking.

Oh my god. I step back.

This isn't a friend.

I bolt out the door. I fly down a few steps and out into the yard. My bare feet pound on the frozen earth. There's a driveway that goes out into the trees, and I run for it.

I hear him hoot, "We've got a runner, Jayden!"

Adrenaline spurs in my blood. I barely see the trees as they fly past. I need to go faster, harder. I'm barely breathing as I fly.

I hear heavy footsteps behind me.

"Better run, little one. You won't like it when I catch you."

The voice isn't familiar. And it's close.

I pant out a tiny scream and veer off into the trees. Instantly, I'm whipped in the face by a small branch. I power through, running along a small gulley. I step on something sharp and briefly register pain, but then it's gone. I jump over a fallen log. I feel myself slowing as my lungs scream for air, and I desperately pump my arms and try to go faster.

Footsteps crash behind me right before strong arms band around me. I go flying toward the ground, but at the last minute, I'm flipped and land on a hard body. We slide to a stop. I thrash, kick, punch, and scrabble for contact. I'm flipped again, and a large body presses me into the earth. I look into the wild eyes of the stranger.

He gives a predatory grin. "Caught you."

I scream out a feral cry and try to scoot away. He presses his pelvis into me. He's rock-hard. And huge.

The man reaches down and cups my core.

With horror, I realize I'm wet. He also realizes the same thing. His blue eyes flash to mine, his pupils dilated. He rips his hand from my pelvis and grips my jaw, squeezing so hard my teeth cut into my cheeks, and I'm forced to open.

"You're so hot when you're afraid."

He hovers over me and spits into my mouth.

A gush of wetness floods my core.

"Now, now, don't devour my prize just yet, Cole," A bored voice sounds above us. Fingers dig into my jaw, forcing it to shut. I look up and see him standing there, arms crossed.

"Swallow, little one," The blond man, Cole, says. I debate spitting, but he digs his fingers in harder. I whimper and swallow. Cole stands up. "Whatever you say, Jay."

The loss of body heat hits me, and I shiver. My gaze darts around.

"No, no, enough running." Jayden lifts me up by my arm and

throws me over his shoulder. "Cole will be balls deep in you before you can get another twenty feet."

"She wouldn't complain."

I gasp. My feet scream in pain. I'm trying to wrap my mind around what just happened.

"You got her to shut up. I'm going to have to get you to chase her down more often." Jayden rumbles a laugh as he walks with me.

Cole growls, "Let me fuck her next time. The speechless factor is much more potent."

Jayden smacks my ass, and I cry out as the old bruise flares. "What did I tell you, kitten? Run and you will be punished. I'm going to let Cole help."

I shiver, the cold seeping along my skin. But I don't fight to get away. My brain is in a haze, and I taste spearmint from Cole's mouth.

We make it back to the house.

"She's bleeding, Jay."

Am I? I try to right myself, and it earns me another smack on the ass.

He places me down on the couch. "Sit still." Jayden grabs my right foot. I look to see that it's dripping blood, a nasty gash by my toes. The pain hits me in a wave, and I close my eyes.

I open my eyes to see Cole also crouched on the floor next to me. It strikes me how handsome he is as well. His jawline is sharp, and his eyes are bright. His eyes twinkle. "So you're good with spit, but blood is a no-go?"

I feel like I got hit by a freight train. My chest hurts, and I can't feel my fingers. I try to flip him the bird. It takes effort.

He laughs.

"It might need stitches."

I jerk my upper body forward. "No. Fuck no." No needles. I try to pull my foot to me, but Jayden pins my shin against the couch.

"Cole, grab the first aid kit."

Cole gives a mock salute and moves to another area of the cabin.

I tremble. Jayden must feel it because he looks up at me. For a brief second, his eyes are unfiltered, and I think I see...concern? Then they shutter down again, and it's like it was never there. Maybe it wasn't.

Cole returns with a military-style duffle bag and rips it open. Gauze, tape, and bottles are inside, along with a bunch of other things. This isn't an ordinary plastic red kit.

"Who are you guys?" I look between them.

"I'm your wet dream." Cole winks at me. Jayden huffs. Cole sees me eyeing the medical-grade equipment.

"What, Jay didn't tell you he commandeered the good shit when he was a cop?"

I freeze. My entire body locks up.

Jayden shoots Cole a dark look. "Sharing is over. Give me the peroxide."

Cole raises his eyebrows, looking surprised.

A cop? This man was a cop? They get to cleaning my cut methodically, like they've done it before.

Dread pools in my stomach. I'm so fucked. I am so fucked. I was counting on the cops to find me. Are they still his buddies? Would they turn a blind eye?

I don't realize I'm hyperventilating until Cole pats my knee. "All done. For now, we'll hold off on the stitches and see how it heals. This is why you don't go running without shoes, even if the big bad wolf comes to your door." He winks and leans into me, whispering, "But I'll chase you anytime."

I shiver. Jayden never gave me shoes. I start to say something, but Jayden stands and swoops me up, bridal style. I'm so surprised I grip his shirt. His smell of musk and oil overwhelms me. He carries me into my room and lays me on the bed. "Punishment later. For now, rest." He cuffs me and leaves the room, shutting the door.

I roll to my side, all fight gone. My body tries again to flip between the feelings of arousal and hate and confusion and panic. It's a dizzying cycle. A sudden wave of defeat rolls through me. I'm so tired.

Fuck Jayden. And fuck Cole too. How dare they steal me from my life, friends, and everything I know? I miss Carissa, I miss Kyle, I miss my house, I miss my goddamn bed. They'll be sick with worry. Kyle probably thinks I'm dead. I might be soon. I wonder if I'll make one of those Dateline shows. Man stalks social media influencer, kidnaps and kills her. The media would have a hay day.

I let myself wallow in self-pity until I fall asleep.

I OPEN MY EYES. My foot throbs like a bitch, and anger rolls through me again, the emotion an old friend at this point. I welcome it like a mother hen, pushing away all the other things I felt last night. Anger is good. Anger will keep me safe. It will keep me alive.

My door opens, and Jayden comes in and gives me a disgusted look.

Game on, motherfucker.

He lets me use the bathroom. When I emerge into the hallway, he and Cole sit on stools at the kitchen island, eating. It smells like bacon, and my mouth waters. I begin limping that way, but Jayden cuts me a blistering look.

"Walking is for good girls who don't break the rules. On your knees."

I freeze, glaring at him. We stare at each other. He drums his finger on the table. "Don't make me ask again, kitten."

"I'm not a kitten. I'm a human being."

Cole looks over at me. Jayden's gaze darkens. "Would you prefer I call you pet? Put a collar on that pretty little neck? Yank you around by a leash?"

"I'm not normally into pet play." Cole has stopped eating and is watching me closely. "But her skin would pinken nicely with a little correction, wouldn't it?"

I curl my lip and slowly get on my knees.

Cole turns to Jayden. "Not house-trained yet, I see?"

Jayden grunts, "She has the manners of a feral cat."

They go back to eating. I glare at both of them. Cole winks at me.

"Crawl," Jayden demands.

"What?" I growl.

"Crawl." He leans back with a satisfied look on his face.

My face burns. Fuck this goddamned fucker. I cuss him out in my head as I drop to my hands and begin crawling. The skin between my bones and the floor is thin. The room goes deadly silent.

I look up.

Both men have stopped what they're doing and are staring at me with raw hunger in their eyes. It makes the blood rush to my core.

Fuck. I didn't want to like this. I couldn't like this. I lick my lips against my dry mouth.

There's the telltale click of a picture being taken. Jayden has a phone out and looks at me with cruel, cold eyes.

I get to the legs of the table and move to stand. Jayden growls, "Did I tell you to get up? You'll stay on your knees in front of me until I say to move."

I freeze and glare at him. I imagine sawing his balls off with floss, stuffing that phone into his mouth, and breaking his teeth.

He smiles and motions near his thigh. "Stay."

I open my mouth to say something and then stop. Fine. I'll

just take it and move on. In the grand scheme of things, he's not hurting me.

Both men eat in charged silence.

Cole reaches down and hands me a small piece of bacon.

I bristle.

He continues holding it to me.

My stomach rumbles. Fine. Fine. I reach out to grab it, and he jerks it away.

"Mouth, pretty girl."

He wants me to eat out of his hand? Like a dog? I jerk my stare up at him and then look at Jayden. His eyes have gone black, his pupils blown.

At that moment, I see an opportunity. It's stupid, but I take it. I lean over and close my mouth around two of Cole's fingers and the bacon. I use my tongue on the back of his knuckles and sensually, slowly pop off of him with the bacon in my mouth, all while watching Jayden.

Jayden's eyes shift from controlled to...something else. He growls and snatches me up, sitting me on the barstool next to him.

"Jesus Christ, that was hot." Cole slowly looks me up and down. He flexes his fingers, making the tanned skin on his forearms ripple.

Jayden stands, throwing his paper plate in the trash, and stalks out of the room.

Cole grins, "I think you broke him."

I found something that shattered his tightly held control. In my head, I dance around. It's the first excitement I've felt since I was taken. I keep my face impassive. Score one for Jo, fucker. I reach across the table to get another piece of bacon.

"How's your foot?"

I glance up at him and stop chewing. "Why would you care?"

He stares at me, then voices lower, "Why wouldn't I?" He looks at me like I'm a puzzle he's trying to solve.

"It's fine," I lie.

Jayden doesn't emerge from wherever he went for the rest of the morning. Cole is staying in the basement as far as I can tell, and occasionally, he'll bring a satellite phone up and go outside for a call. I convince him to show me his room downstairs. There's a game room with a pool table, and his bedroom is off to the side. In it, there's a desk with paperwork and a computer that looks like it's from the early 2000s. As well as old baseball posters on the walls.

"So, is that how you met Jayden? Being a cop?" We've moved upstairs and are sitting in the living room. I'm pretending to read a book, and he's whittling a piece of wood.

He grunts, "Hardly."

"How then?"

"We knew each other as kids."

"Just decided to become kidnapping assholes together then, or what?"

He laughs like I told a joke. When he stops, he looks at me above his wood and asks, "Are you trying to get to know him through me?"

I look up at him. Mirth sparkles in his eyes, but they also have a sharp, cunning edge.

"I think you really like him."

I sputter, then laugh. I laugh and laugh and laugh. And then something horrifying happens. I realize I don't have the ability to like someone anymore. That choice was ripped away from me. I liked Kyle, and it was taken from me, and suddenly, it seems like the saddest thing in the world.

Tears well in my eyes, and I try to push them back, but one slips loose, and I choke on a breath. The choke does me in, and I start sobbing. Oh my god. Getting kidnapped, beaten, and humiliated wasn't enough to break me, but this is?

Cole stands and walks over to me, rubbing the back of his neck. "You okay?"

"F-fine." I can't stop the tears, and I hate myself for it. Why the fuck can't I stop?

Cole sits next to me, shifts, then rubs my back awkwardly. That simple gesture makes me cry more. I hide my face in my hands.

"What the fuck did you do to her?" an angry voice demands.

"Nothing dude, I said I think she has a crush on you, and then this!"

"Snap out of it, Mary." Strong hands land on my wrists.

"Fuck you." I push Jayden away, looking at the floor, and try so hard not to cry that I silently hiccup. I get up, walk to my room, and slam the door.

I cry for a while longer. I cry until I remember what I stole earlier from Cole's desk.

I pull a paperclip out of my bra. I hold it like it's as fragile as a baby bird. Then, I tuck it up between the mattress and the box spring.

## JAYDEN

8

---

Normally, tears get me hard. I don't know what the fuck is wrong with me because those tears made me feel something else entirely.

I shift and look back at the picture of her crawling toward me.

Sage will be so mad when I send it to her.

"Can you send that picture to me when you get a chance?" Cole looks up at me.

"Sure."

"God, dude, I know I said it before, but she's a hottie." He adjusts himself. "Surely you guys have done it on every surface in here already. Don't lie."

I glare at the phone screen, wiping off smudges.

He notices my silence and sits up a little straighter. "You haven't?"

I drum my fingers on the couch.

"Okay, just your room?" He smiles.

"No, Cole."

His face drops, and he gets that calculating look. "What the fuck? Isn't that what she signed up for?"

"She didn't sign up for anything."

He looks confused. "Your kink app?"

"That's not a thing."

He stares at me, his mind working. I see the second he looks at the scratch on my face, and his eyes widen a fraction. Anger rolls across his face, and his voice gets lower. "Why is she here, Jay?"

I cross my arms and stare at him.

"Holy fuck." He leans in. "She joked about us being kidnappers...but that wasn't a joke?"

I lift a brow.

"You took a woman, then brought her to my cabin, and I almost fucked her as she fought?"

"You didn't, though."

"I was going to until you came along!" He runs a hand through his blond hair and lets out a short breath. "I can't believe this." He pauses. "Did you leave any way for them to track you here?"

"Of course not," I snap.

His eyes show slight relief. He sits quietly for what feels like forever, just sitting. When he speaks, his voice is quiet. "You're doing to her what happened to us."

Dark anger instantly clouds my vision. "This is not the same."

"Not the same?" he whisper-yells. "Our choice was taken away. You're taking away her choice. For what, a little revenge?"

"She wants it; you can see it in her eyes." I know he's seen the open lust she looks at us with.

"Jesus Christ, dude, you're fucked up." He paces away and to the kitchen, snatching a banana.

"Are you with me?" I look at him, hating seeing a glimpse of that familiar haunted look in his eyes. Hating that I put it there.

"Of course, I'm with you." He rips it open and gestures to me with it. "Give me half a second to bury what's left of my god-damned morals, for Christ's sake."

I let out a breath. He had always been there for me. We would always be with each other. He may not understand what I'm doing yet, but he will. I'll make sure of it.

I pulled up the screenshot I took of Mary from *the* video. I had stared at it for hours. Mesmerized. Angry. Hateful. Intrigued.

"So, what are we doing with her?"

It is time to continue the plan.

# Mary Jo

9

My foot feels a little better. It has scabbed over and doesn't look quite so angry and red. I still have no shoes or socks though, so walking is a pain in my ass. Which upsets the shit out of me. I'll need to bide my time.

I spend hours in my room, reading a book I had taken from the living room, and watching the sun trace patterns on the walls. I expect Jayden to bother me, but he doesn't speak one word to me all day. Even when I leave my room to get food. My frozen meals are running low. Instead, I stick to peanut butter sandwiches, bringing them back to my room. Cole isn't around. Either that, or he is laying low.

I listen to the sounds of the house, keeping inventory of what time Jayden does what. Well, as well as I can guess the time.

When evening rolls around, I can't sleep. Jayden doesn't come in to lock me up. I toss and turn until I fall into a fitful sleep.

I wake up with the feeling that I'm not alone.

I start up in bed, seeing two massive forms standing at the end of it wearing masks. The masks are white with holes in them for the eyes and mouth. One has a ghost smile in it, and the other has a slit for the mouth and stitching over the eyes. The one with stitching is on my left, and the smiling face is on my right.

"Hello, pretty girl." I can't tell who growls it. Their voice is low and angry. "Care to play?"

I jump to my feet.

They toss a small black item down on my bed.

"You have 60 seconds to run. If you get away for longer than five minutes, we won't put this on you."

I can't tell what it is, but it doesn't matter. I bolt.

The one in the smiling mask reaches out and yanks a piece of my hair as I go by.

I sprint past the bathroom and to the front door. They've left it unlocked. I shoot out into the night and run around the house to the garage. There's a fine layer of frost all over everything.

I need to hide and wait them out. I only have 60 seconds, and they're both much faster than me.

The garage has two garage doors and one wooden one. It's unlocked. I bolt inside and slam the door, locking the deadbolt and door knob. I stand in the dark, blind for a second. To my left are a truck and a car. The garage is two stories with what looks like an open balcony and a shop upstairs.

Think Jo! They'll know this garage better than me. I need something to give me the upper hand.

I spot a cinder block to my right. I grab it and run upstairs, heart pounding, heaving for air. There's a workbench near the railing, and I crawl up into the bottom shelf. Then I wait.

I try to get my breathing under control, but it feels like I can't catch my breath.

My time has to be up by now. I picture both of them coming for me, stalking me. It does weird things to my core, and I realize with horror that I'm turned on.

Something is terribly wrong with me.

The door downstairs rattles.

I hunker down more.

There's a pause, and then the deadbolt slams open, and the door slowly squeaks open. I look through the cracked cabinet doors of the bench. A man stands in the doorway, silhouetted by the icy frost behind him. His breath puffs out the top of his mask.

"Come out, come out wherever you are, pet."

I shiver. His dark voice snakes right to my center. It sounds like he wants to devour me. He saunters in, and the other steps in behind him. They walk casually to the stairs.

Fuck! I needed them to walk under the balcony.

Their footsteps come in measured scrapes against the stairs. Scrape. Scrape. Scrape.

Then nothing. Complete silence.

I hold my breath. My pulse pounds in my ears. I wait. And wait. I close my eyes.

My cabinet doors fling open.

"Hello, kitten," the voice purrs.

A terrifying white mask with dark holes is face to face with me.

I scream. I scramble past him, and he steps out of the way. I don't register that that's a problem before I slam into a hard body.

Arms band around me, pinning me.

"What time you got?"

"Two minutes. Tsk tsk, we gotta work on that time, kitten."

I scream and struggle. The arms clamp harder, restricting my movement and even my breathing.

"Fighting turns me on, little one," the voice warns. I'm pretty sure it's Cole, but I can't tell for sure.

My hands are down at my sides. I pause for a second to breathe.

"What were you going to do with this cinder block, hmmm? Thinking about breaking one of the rules?"

I use my good foot to rake down the shin of the man holding me while I jerk my hand around to grab his junk. I squeeze through the heavy cargo material and twist.

With a pained grunt, he lets me go.

I fly down the stairs. I briefly notice bloody footprints on them. My footprints. That's how they found me so quickly.

Footsteps sprint close behind me, and a shadow pushes past me to block the door. I veer to the vehicle and jump over the hood of the car.

I'm snatched up again and tossed into the bed of the truck. I scramble to get up, but the smiling mask is on me, hand against my throat, as he pins me to the back of the cab.

He laughs with no hint of humor. "You asked for it."

I scrabble at his hands, but it only makes him tighten his grip. Sounds go mute against my ears, and my eyes start to close.

I don't realize he's loosened his hold until I hear the other jump into the bed of the truck. I renew my clawing until smiley breathes in my ear, "Be still, or I'll put you out. He has something to say to you."

I look into the eyes of the masked man who crouches in front of me. They're dark, as far as I can see.

"Things have been way too relaxed recently. There are new rules." He traces a finger along my lips.

I shiver.

"First. This mouth gets shitty with us, it gets punished. I'll show you what it means to have a mouth full of filth."

He adjusts his cock.

I gasp, realizing what he means.

He takes the opportunity to slide two fingers into my mouth. He shoves them all the way back until I gag.

I bite down hard.

He pulls out and smacks my cheek so hard I see stars. The hand around my throat doesn't let up. I get even more wet.

"That's the last time those pretty teeth will bite me. Ever. You understand?"

I nod, blinking away involuntary tears from the slap.

"Two. If we're playing, you call me Sir. That's the only way you'll address me. You'll call him Master." It must be Jayden in the mask with a slit for a mouth. He nods at what must be Cole pinning my throat.

"The old rules still apply unless either of us tells you to run, you don't hurt us, you don't run. If you fuck up, you crawl the rest of the day. As well as anything else we decide."

I'm pinching my thighs together.

He notices.

"Three. You never touch yourself unless we tell you to."

I suck in a breath. What the hell?

Smiley leans in. "You can always beg me to do it for you...and I'll think about it. If you're a good girl."

I shake my head and grit, "I'll never do something like that, mother—"

Jayden grabs the button on the top of his pants.

I remember the rule and stop.

"What do you call him?"

I grit my teeth as wetness pools in my core against my will. "Master."

"Thank me for not punishing you for that outburst."

"Thank you very much..." I can't keep a slight mocking out of my voice.

"She doesn't learn."

The hand tightens on my throat. "Nope."

"It's all pretty simple." He leans his mask into my face. "Lower your pants."

My eyes flare, and I jerk to get away, but I'm pinned solidly.

"Don't act shy now. We told you the rules." He takes a deep breath, seeming to feed on my fear.

Pressure is building in my core, and everything feels hot. I slide my hand down to my leggings and push them down a little.

"All the way."

I do.

I feel the predatory hunger from both men and suddenly become aware of the pounding heartbeat in my clit.

"Play with yourself."

The words make heat flame across my cheeks. I feel exposed, but something about their ragged breathing turns me on even more.

"I've never...done this...like this."

Dangerous silence.

"Sir."

He leans in, his voice rumbling behind the mask. "You're going to touch that pretty little cunt. You're going to make it drip for us. So you know you belong to us."

I dip a finger down under my panties to brush against my clit. It feels so good I swallow against the hand on my neck.

I glance to my right. Two burning blue eyes look back at me.

I swipe over my clit again, and a wave of pleasure runs through me. Normally it takes a few minutes of play or porn, but I'm so turned on right now I feel electric.

There's a soft moan beside me.

Jayden pulls out a phone and points it at me.

I yank my hand back.

"If you stop, I'll send this to Kyle."

Holy shit, Kyle. A wave of shame fills me. I'm touching myself in front of two other men while he's probably frantically looking for me.

A strong finger drums on my neck. "Focus, little one."

Jayden keeps facing the phone at me, his eyes hard. Embarrassment is hot in my body, but my core hasn't gotten the message. The more I think I shouldn't do this, the more wet I become.

Slowly, I dip my hand back again. I circle my clit, feeling the arousal dripping out of me. The hand tightens. Pleasure and hatred create a headiness in me, and a soft moan slips out.

"Fuck." It's Cole.

I close my eyes and keep going.

"Eyes open," Jayden snaps. "On me. I want you to look at me as you pleasure that dirty cunt."

I open them again. He stares me down while I play. I do my best to glare back. Electric tingles shoot in waves from my core, and my muscles clench. I feel myself get wetter as sounds start to fuzz from the pressure on my neck. I jerk my hips up to meet my fingers. I'm slipping closer and closer into a spiral of pleasure as dark eyes stare back at me.

Just as I'm about to come, a loud voice demands, "Stop."

I let out a frustrated cry. The hand releases me. My inner muscles flutter, needing release.

"Only good girls get to come. And you are not one." Jayden pulls something out of his pocket, and before I can react, slips it around my ankle and locks it together.

I look down.

An ankle monitor.

A goddamn ankle monitor.

Fire fills my blood. I spit, "Your mother never loved you, did she?"

He laughs, and the sound is full of menace, "No, kitten. She didn't." He leans into me, and his breath comes hot through the mask. "The sooner you get this, the better things will go for you. You belong to me. You belong to him. We control the very air you breathe. Your orgasms. Where you go and what you do. You'll be our good little pet, or we'll punish you. And punishments only get worse from here."

I growl, shame and anger fill me, "I hate you, *Sir*." More than I've ever hated anyone.

He laughs and throws the mask off his face, his dark hair tousled, his cheekbones catching the low light. "You have no idea. I haven't scratched the surface of what I'm going to do to you."

Jayden stands.

"Help her back, Cole." He looks at me in disgust. "That foot needs to be looked at again."

He drops down from the bed of the truck and disappears.

Cole slides the mask off his face and holds out a hand to me.

"I got it," I snap, then follow with a mocking, "Master."

He chuckles.

I pull my leggings back up, realizing how exposed I am. I stand and also realize how much I'm bleeding. Running must have opened the cut more.

Cole turns his back to me and crouches down.

"Hop on."

A piggyback ride? Jesus, what dimension am I in? I'm getting whiplash from their mood changes. I consider refusing but know that'll get me in more trouble. I hesitantly wrap my legs around his back. I grab only as much of his shoulders and chest as I need to keep from falling off. He gets us out of the truck and walks us out of the garage. He walks like I weigh nothing.

He's warm and muscled under me. We walk back to the cabin. Once inside, he sets me on the kitchen island and puts in the code in the alarm box.

I watch, but he uses his body to shield what he's doing.

He returns.

The sound of a car engine sounds from outside.

He puts both his hands on the outsides of my thighs. "He's going to town to get more supplies. Just you and me, lemon drop."

I glare at the stupid name.

"Lemon, cause your hair." He gestures at my blond, "And because you're tart. I like it."

"I hate it."

He ducks his head into my neck and takes a deep breath through his nose. "Noted. I'll take it up with management. Now give me your foot."

He bandages me up again. It hurts more than last time. When he's done, he goes upstairs. He comes back down with a small pill.

"For the pain."

I eye it, then him.

He shrugs. "I'm not going to make you take it. But keep in mind I don't need to drug you to do what I want with you, little one."

With that, he picks me up, puts me on the couch, and pulls a blanket over me. He flips off all the lights but the bear lampshade on the end table. He then flips his knife out of his back pocket and gets to whittling again on the couch across from me.

Pain and exhaustion hit me at once. I debate not taking the pill just to prove a point, but pain wins out, and I grab a water bottle from the coffee table and take it. I try to keep my eyes open, but I soon fall fast asleep.

IN THE BATHROOM the next morning, I examine the ankle monitor on my left leg. It's tight to my skin, but not uncomfortably so. I try to remember what I've seen about ankle monitors on TV. Aren't they super hard to get off? This one looks like it's just attached by a thin strip of rubber. But on TV, as soon as you messed with them, the cops got a notification.

Don't they require some sort of service to work? I wonder if he would put it on me when it doesn't work just to fuck with me.

Probably.

Jayden comes back sometime mid-morning. I sit around in my room, pretending to read. I'm still horny from the night before. I want to touch myself, but I'm paranoid that he'll know somehow. But that thought also makes me horny.

Which makes me angry.

I need a distraction. Desperately.

I limp to the kitchen. It's just Jayden relaxing in the living room. I look in the fridge and see some new groceries.

I clear my throat. Jayden doesn't look up. I do it again, louder. He cocks an eyebrow at me.

I picture smacking him in his pretty face but keep my tone neutral. "Can I cook?"

He arches a dark eyebrow. "I don't know, can you?"

I huff, "Yes. I *can*. I'm asking permission." Annoying asshole.

He stands and walks over. I look up at him and cross my arms. Pretend like he didn't see my pussy last night. Like I didn't like it.

"How bad do you want to, kitten?"

I close my eyes and swallow. "Badly."

"Beg."

I look up into his face. All traces of relaxation are gone, and he's hard and emotionless again.

I purse my lips. "Please."

He looks bored. "Did you even try?"

I huff. Then, ever so slowly, get on my knees. I look up at him and put my hands on his thighs. He tenses at the touch. I lift my gaze to him. In a low voice and tone barely above a whisper, I ask, "Please...Sir."

I can't help but feel warm and tingly at my embarrassment and the proximity of my face to his crotch.

He grabs my chin and forces me to look at his face. "Yes. You may cook." He drops his hold and stalks away, leaving me on my knees.

I scramble up. When I'm sure he's facing away, I flip him off and then turn back to the fridge.

I spend the next hour scrounging together what I can with limited ingredients. I did find glass spice jars tucked on a top shelf. I made a hamburger curry with hamburger buns and frozen green beans. I had to sit down periodically as my foot was killing me. Whatever Cole gave me last night had worn off, but cooking felt good. For the first time since being taken, I felt like myself. I didn't realize how badly I missed feeling like me. And that made me sad.

I make enough for all of us. Cole came up from downstairs, and the men talk while I keep silent. I do the dishes. Cole sees me favoring my foot and brings me another pill, which I take immediately. Everyone then relaxes on the couches for a while like some fucked up group of friends.

Jayden has been too neutral since eating. He hasn't even sent me a disgusted look. I have a feeling this truce will be over the minute the sun goes down.

I'M RIGHT.

I go to my room to try and avoid it, but two shadows stalk in. They stand at the end of my bed with their arms crossed.

"Did you touch yourself today?"

I pull my legs up to my chest. "No."

Jayden gives me a long stare. "Did you want to?"

My cheeks get hot, and I hate myself for it. "No."

Cole leans in. "Don't lie to us, pretty girl." His voice is not at all like it normally is. It's low and full of promise.

"Yes," I whisper.

Cole straightens and leaves the room. I panic. Jayden comes around the bed and cuffs me to it. I try to fight him, but he bats my hands back like they're annoying flies.

Cole comes back in with what looks like an old laptop. He opens it, and some movie is pulled up on the screen.

No, not a movie. Porn. And I recognize the actors. They're the ones I always watch. My gaze jumps to Jayden. "How—"

He presses play, and a loud female moan fills the room. Ass is on full display on the screen as the male mounts behind the bound woman.

"You nasty girl. Do you like how he roughs her up? Takes what's his?"

I put my hands on my burning cheeks. The sounds of wet flesh slapping on wet flesh begin, so loud in the small room.

Cole places the laptop on the edge of my bed.

Jayden says, "Don't move it, don't touch it, and don't touch yourself."

They stalk out of the room.

I stare at the laptop, eyes wide. It feels dirty that they know what I watch, like something very private is being blasted all over social media.

The male actor has switched from pounding the woman's pussy from behind to eating her out. She's bound on the bed, hands stretched above her so she can't stop him. She moans loudly.

Embarrassment fights with my horniness. The shame is overwhelming.

I close my eyes. This will be fine. I won't let them win this. Everyone watches porn. There is nothing to be embarrassed about.

As I ease my embarrassment and listen to the sounds of fucking though, my horniness rises. Grunting and soft gasps of pleasure. Some slaps of pain. Knowing she can't get away while he claims her.

No! I need to stop this.

It is something to be embarrassed about. They know your

fantasies. They shouldn't know. You're an embarrassment. They think you're sick. What would Kyle think?

*They like sick.*

Fuck.

I look at the computer again. It's the first time I've had access to an electronic since I was taken. Surely they wouldn't leave me with access to the internet?

But how else was the video playing? It looked just like it did when I played it on my phone.

Little warning bells go off in my head, saying I have yet to beat them in their own game. Fuck them. I move the mouse and see that I can make the existing screen smaller without turning it off. I click to do so. I look at the toolbar but don't see internet access.

Fuck.

I click the video back to full screen.

The video ends, and another one starts. And then that one ends, and another one starts. Over and over. The volume is up very loud. Spankings and punishments and orgasms.

My panties are soaked. I've given up trying to not be horny and just accept it.

My door bursts open, and I jump.

Both men come in. They have t-shirts on, so their muscled and tattooed arms are clearly visible. They look dangerous.

They did that on purpose.

Cole takes the computer, and the sounds of fucking finally stop. He clicks around for a bit, and my heart rate speeds up. What is he looking for?

Jayden watches me.

"Can't follow rules, hmmm, pretty girl?" Cole snaps the computer shut.

"What? I didn't—"

"You know Cole can see if you clicked on anything, right?"

Fuck.

"I think she just wants punishment, Jay."

"I didn't break your stupid, goddamned rules!"

But they aren't paying me any attention.

Jayden grabs my hair and pulls me off the bed, forcing me to my knees. He faces me toward Cole while unlocking my wrist. He leans down, and his breath is hot in my ear. "You're going to take his dick out, and then you're going to suck it. You're going to be our good little whore, and you're going to touch yourself while you do it."

I whimper. Then I hate how weak I sound, and I snarl, "Fuck you."

Jayden yanks my head back to look at him. He's smiling. "That's the point, kitten."

He keeps his hand in my hair while he shoves me toward Cole.

I glare at Cole while my clit forms a heartbeat. He looks down at me and flashes his white teeth in a grin that doesn't reach his eyes. He unzips his jeans.

"Suck, pretty girl."

The hand in my hair jerks me toward him again, so tight in my strands it makes tears come to my eyes. I squirm, pressing my thighs together as Cole pulls his dick out.

It's big. And smooth, with veins running up and down it. There's a drop of precum at the tip.

"Open." Jayden digs his other hand into my jaw, and I'm forced to open.

Cole shoves into my mouth while Jayden pushes me onto him, and I immediately gag. He pulls back and shoves in again. I cough and try to sputter. This time, when he pulls back, he slows, allowing me to get accommodated.

I know how to give blowies. It used to be the only way Kyle would have sex with me. I debate if I want to make it good for him. I look up and see Cole's pupils blown out.

I flatten my tongue and suck.

"God," he growls.

Tingles run across my skin. I bring my hands up to his dick, but I get a sharp jerk on my hair.

"I said play with yourself. I want you to come thinking about how full we could make you."

I drop my right hand down and continue to suck. I use my left hand to squeeze the base of his dick and slurp up and down. I put my hand down my pants and moan at how good it feels.

Cole moans, too.

"Hear that? Hear how good you're making him feel?" Jayden growls. "That's a good little slut."

I lick around his tip while playing with myself, then slide him into the back of my throat. I relax and swallow him down.

"Jesus," Cole stutters, his hips clearly wanting to take over but holding back. I bob on him, then pull back to take in a breath. I go back in, swallowing him down again, this time playing with his balls.

He releases his restraint and starts fucking my mouth and throat hard. I look up, tears leaking out of my eyes and snot coming out of my nose. The cordial Cole is no longer there. His eyes are hard and angry. He looks feral.

My clit throbs as I rub fast. All the pent-up desire from yesterday and today fills my veins. I've never been so turned on. Pleasure floods me, and I groan, my eyes rolling back in my head.

"You gonna come, kitten?" Jayden growls in my ear. It takes effort, but I flip him off with the finger around Cole's dick. He chuckles darkly.

Cole hasn't let me take a breath, and things are starting to feel fuzzy and full of pleasure. I rub faster, and the pleasure builds and builds.

"Come for us, pretty whore."

Lightning streaks through me, and all my muscles tense. I come hard and cry out around his dick.

I'm vaguely aware of Cole also shouting and jerking. Warmth spills down my throat. I swallow as my inner muscles pulse over and over.

"Fuck." He pulls out of my mouth, and I gasp in a breath. I heave for oxygen, and the hand in my hair releases.

"Fuck she was too good, I had to come."

Pleasure still fogs my mind. I hear movement, but I just sit still and float in the haze. Part of me notices someone crouching in front of me and picking me up. There's movement and stairs, and I hear a shower turn on.

A shower! I haven't showered since I got here. I blink and find myself and Cole in a small bathroom with a standup shower, the water steaming.

"Holy fuck," I breathe. I strip my clothes and hop in. The water feels glorious, and I feel like I've gone to heaven as hot streams cut down my body. I stand in the stream for a long time, soaking away all the grime. The bandage on my foot gets soaked, and still I stand some more.

"There's soap on the shelf."

I jump. I forgot Cole was in here. He leans back against the sink, arms crossed, watching me.

I reach for it and scrub myself down. I don't want to leave the shower. Clarity is beginning to come back, and when I leave, I know I'll have to face reality.

"You can go now," I tell him.

"You look like you're going to fall asleep standing up. No."

I turn away so he doesn't see my nakedness as easily. The water begins to cool, and I cover my breasts and look for a towel.

He hands me one, and I wrap myself up and stare at him.

"Piss off, pretty boy."

His look shifts from hunger to darkness. "What was that little one?" He looks like he'll jam his cock down my throat again, and I swallow, too sore for that.

"Please leave. I'm going to get dressed."

"I just saw you naked. It's a little late for that."

"Leave!" Tears fill my eyes, and I blink them away in anger.

He pauses for a second, then leaves.

I quickly dress and then take a deep breath. I stalk out of the bathroom and up the stairs, holding it together until I shut my door. My room still smells of sex.

I thought I'd cry, but all my emotions shut down when I get into bed. I stare blankly at the wall, not feeling anything.

I stare like that for a while, then lie down and close my eyes. I'm not sure when I fall asleep.

## 10

Watching her suck Cole off was a heaven I didn't know existed. Her pretty lips stretched around him, the tears streaming down her face, the noises she made when she came. How she had my friend in ecstasy. The dual hatred and surrender in her eyes.

Intoxicating. I'm obsessed. If I wasn't already.

I can still make it work with my plan. But now I'm keeping her.

She belongs to us.

And I don't think I'll ever let her go.

# COLE

## 11

The hot water pounds over my body, and I lean my forehead against the tile of the shower. I stare at the familiar tiles with their light brown speckles.

Hot breath and grunting fill the room. "What a good boy. Make daddy feel good."

My mouth feels salty. I spit and squeeze my eyes shut, hitting my forehead on the wet tile. That's not real. Not anymore. I'm at the cabin.

Why didn't I think to grab my knife? My skin itches with the need to draw blood. See the pretty red beads well up and erase everything else.

I don't know how long I stand there, but when the door opens, the water is cold.

"Fuck," Jayden says. The water turns off, and he grabs me a towel.

"Fuck off, dude." I shake the water from my hair and yank the towel out of his hand.

He just stands there. It's been a long time since he's found me like this. I can't look at him. I cover up the scars on my back that I know damn well he has too and brush past him to my room.

# Mary Jo

12

I'M TRYING NOT TO THINK ABOUT WHAT HAPPENED LAST night. The shame of coming for people who kidnapped me, of loving it and their words.

If anything, it makes me hate them more.

I need to get out of here. The problem is there are two of them. I need to get rid of one of them if I'm to even have any hope of overpowering the other. I have my sights set on Cole's whittling knife and the car keys. I haven't seen where they keep the keys or even heard them take them out of their pockets. I'm guessing they're in the garage. Cole must keep his knife downstairs when it isn't on him.

I also need shoes. It's cold as fuck outside, and my cut keeps slowing me down.

"Did you ever get that ATV fixed?" I'm in the kitchen making pancakes. Jayden looks at me from perusing the fridge.

"No." He cocks an eyebrow and shuts the fridge.

"I can help." I flip a pancake.

He narrows his eyes.

"I'm bored as fuck all day. I'm not trying to run. I used to help my dad with stuff like that."

He knows I grew up on a farm. He did his research on me for whatever reason. I can see him run through a bunch of different reasons I'd offer. Finally, he says, "Fine."

"I promise. You can cuff me to you if you really think I'm going to run." I put a stack of pancakes on a plate.

"I can cuff you anytime I want, kitten."

The morning stretches on. Neither men mention work or jobs. Surely two men in their thirties have to work sometime? But I don't ask. Cole hangs out downstairs and whittles upstairs while shooting the shit with Jayden. They appear totally relaxed. Dicks.

I'm anxious to go to the garage, but I don't push it. Finally, in the late afternoon, Jayden gets up and walks past me to the door. "Let's go. See what you got."

I scramble up from the couch. He doesn't offer me shoes, and by the time we walk across the frozen ground to the garage, my feet hurt. He has the ATV parked under the balcony.

"Can't get her to start up."

"Hmmm." I go to it and begin to look at it, quickly falling into a rhythm from when Dad and I used to tinker around. Jayden and I go back and forth, theorizing and testing certain things. He goes from being skeptical to having an open conversation with me.

The shop lights bathe over his arms and shoulders, reminding me how muscled they are. I also get a closer look at his tattoos. He has tribal swirls up his right arm in a full sleeve, and on his left are pocket watches, dates, and what looks like a wolf on his shoulder under his shirt sleeve. One of the dates on his arm looks fresh. It's dated the 22nd of November. I realize it must be close to the 22nd today, so it's only three months old.

"What's that for?" I point at his arm.

He looks down. Something flashes across his face, but he says in an emotionless tone. "My mother."

Oh. Shit.

I see the problem in the ATV quickly. Jayden keeps brushing his hand over it but doesn't seem to realize.

"I don't know. We might have to try again later. My dad had a model similar to this one a few years ago. I can't remember working on it much, though. Give me a little to think about it." I wipe my hands on a rag and give him my best naive girl look.

He glances at me, then back at the ATV, brows furrowed. He hesitates and then runs a hand through his dark hair. He looks unguarded, and I reluctantly admit how pretty he is. His cheekbones are cut, and his lashes are thick and dark.

He notices me staring. I blush.

"Like what you see, kitten?" He smirks, his face becoming predatory.

I cough. "I'm cold. Let's go inside." I start walking to the door.

He laughs, "Wait."

I barely have time to turn, and he's on me, one hand around the back of my neck and one on my chin. He faces me up to him. I see his black eyes glint, and then he crushes his lips to mine.

He's warm and heavy on me, hands pulling me into his kiss. I part my lips in shock. He takes advantage, swooping his tongue in. He licks and sucks before I have the presence of mind to pull away.

He doesn't let me and continues savaging my mouth. I struggle. He hardly lets me move. I nip at his tongue, but it only deepens the kiss and the pressure, and it feels heavenly. I've never been kissed with such passion. It feels like he's branding my mouth.

He feels me relax into his hold. The hand around my chin drops away, and passion flows into me.

I start to meet his tongue, and then I hear the click of a picture being taken.

I look to my left, and he has the cell phone out. He took a picture of us kissing.

I cry out against his mouth. He's grinning now, looking mean and hungry.

I pull back, and he lets me go.

"You..." I sputter.

"Yes, get nasty with me so I have a reason to punish you again." He tucks the phone back into his pocket.

I want to. I want to punch him in the face. But knowing him, he'd probably laugh and enjoy it. Fuck him. *Fuck him.*

He swoops in and throws me over his shoulder. I beat on his lower back and ass.

"Put me down!"

He ignores me and carts me back to the cabin. I continue uselessly pounding. We get inside, and he doesn't put me down. He carts me upstairs and tosses me on his bed.

I scramble to get up, but he's on me in a flash, pinning my hips down.

He rips my leggings off in one motion, even getting them over the ankle monitor.

"I didn't—I haven't broken a rule!" I cry out.

"This isn't a punishment." He snaps my panties off like they're nothing. I kick to get away, but he spreads my legs apart so my kicks have no force behind them. He drags my ass to the end of the bed.

"Wait!" I struggle and kick.

Hot breath blows against my wet pussy. His shoulder and one arm pin my legs open, and the other arm bands heavily against my waist.

Then his hot mouth is on me. He sucks my clit into his mouth and pulses on it.

I cry out both with the shock of it and the pleasure. He takes advantage of my momentary break in the struggle to open me wider. He releases his suction to lick me from entrance to clit, then buries his nose into me.

He pulls in a deep breath through his nose.

Heat flames in my cheeks. I try to kick again, but he grabs ahold of my clit with his lips and growls, a clear threat.

The vibrations send a shock through my system. I gasp.

He starts to eat me like he's been starving. He licks with the flat of his tongue up and down and up and down with force. He keeps up the same tempo, and my body responds, pushing into him for more.

He instantly stops and starts a different technique and rhythm. Just as it starts to send electricity through my body, he stops and starts something else.

I cry out as anger flows through me. He chuckles against me.

"Well, well, well."

I jump and see Cole smirking at the end of the bed.

Jayden tightens his hold on me and pulls me closer to him, growling deep and low.

Cole laughs, "She's all yours, brother."

"I'm not anyone's!" I start to struggle again. It earns me a sharp nip on the clit. "Ouch!"

His tongue massages away the sting, which only seems to amplify the pleasure.

"Whatever you just did, keep doing it; she likes it."

He bites me again. I can't help it—my body bucks into his mouth. The pain and pleasure feel so good. I keep fighting to hate it. To hate him.

"You look so good spread open for him like that. That pussy is probably getting off knowing you're ours, and there's nothing you can do about it."

I growl at him, "I've had much uglier men get me off quicker." It's a lie, but it hits its mark. His gaze darkens.

Jayden bites me hard, and I feel his teeth dig into my skin. I throw my head back and grit my teeth. He laps at me, and it feels so good I moan. He brings me to the edge of coming again, then backs off. He does it a few more times. My inner muscles are so close to spasming. He licks a finger and puts it inside me, curling up to hit my G spot.

It forces a groan out of me. My thighs try to close around him. I'm so damn close.

I get up on my elbows and try to pull away.

"Fuck no," he snarls. He yanks me into him and starts a hard and consistent pattern on my clit while stroking my G spot.

"You can't fight it, little one," Cole says in a deep husk. "Stop trying."

I kick as sparks fly across my vision. All of my muscles clench down, and blinding pleasure fills me. I clench down in waves on his finger, my body trying to pull him deeper, to make him one with me.

The feeling goes on and on. He keeps at it until he feels my spasming stop.

I pant. I try to push his head away. It's the wrong move. He growls and buries in me again.

I cry out from overstimulation. But soon, pressure builds again, and he wrings another orgasm out of me.

I collapse back on the bed, breathing heavily.

He releases me and crawls over me. I meet his gaze.

"Mine," he growls, eyes burning.

I close my eyes.

He grips my chin, and my eyes startle open again. "*Mine.*" He watches for something, I'm not sure what. I stare back, coming down off adrenaline and pleasure.

He stands, towering over the bed. There's a hard bulge in his pants. Then he turns on his heel and walks downstairs.

I get up on my elbows and watch him go. Cole smirks at me.

I grab the comforter and cover myself.

"That was hot, lemon drop."

All of a sudden, his stupid nickname makes me angry. "That's not my name," I growl.

"Sure it is. You know you open your mouth and make this little cry when you come. It's cute."

I glare at him, and the image of shoving him over the balcony fills my mind.

Cole laughs, and his voice goes lower and deeper. "Whatever murderous thought crossed your little mind, go ahead and try it. We'll fight, and then I'll fill you with my come on his bed."

I stand, pussy hot again, and snatch up the comforter with my torn panties and leggings. I march downstairs.

It's only then that I remember what I saw in the garage. Two sets of keys hung on the wall right by the garage door—keys to the cars.

To give the best odds, I have to wait until sunset to kick-start my plan. It makes me nervous all day the next day. I feel like I'm doing a good job of covering it up, but Jayden keeps giving me long, searching looks.

Still, my plan isn't completely ruined. After dinner, I go to the bathroom and shut the door. I brace my hands on either end of the sink, take a deep breath, and get to work.

A little later, I start crying. At least, I try. For some reason, the tears feel clogged inside, and my emotions feel dry. What the hell? I can cry when it's the most embarrassing, but not when I try to?

I growl. This is gonna hurt like a bitch.

I punch my hand into the mirror. It makes a sharp clank into the wood wall behind it. Pain shoots into my hand.

It doesn't take long. The door handle jiggles, and then a hard thump of a fist.

"Open the door."

I make a strangled sob sound.

"Mary. Open it now."

"Go away!"

"Open, or I'm going to kick it in."

"Jesus Christ." I storm to the door and fling it open. "Can you give a girl some privacy?"

Jayden immediately presses into my personal space. "What was that noise?"

"Nothing." I sniff and ball my hand behind my back.

He notices, and faster than I can react, he's flipped me around and pinned my chest to the wall. He wrenches the thing from my hand.

There's silence, and then he lets me go.

I flip around, and we both look at a bloody pair of my panties. I had to open and re-bandage my foot back up for it.

I press my hands into fists. "You got me, hot shot. Escaping through the walls with nothing but a pair of panties. For Christ's sake, can you not be a horrible person for two seconds and let me have a minute?" My voice rises, shrill now. "Jesus fucking hell, give me a break." I wipe my eyes.

He takes a step back.

"You good?" Cole steps into the doorway. He takes in the scene.

"Fuck." I storm past both of them to my room. They let me go.

I slam the door.

It works like I want it to. Jayden rips it open. "You don't shut my door unless I tell you to."

I hide my face in my hands. "I'm going to bleed all over my clothes! All over the bed."

He's silent for a long time. So long that I peek up.

"I'll get you pads."

I sniff. "And Midol. And chocolate."

He is silent again. He runs a hand through his hair, looking annoyed. Maddeningly, it adds to his handsome appeal.

"Fine. What kind do you want? Long? Heavy flow? Wings?"

I pause. How does he know about women's products? Dread shoots down my spine. Maybe he's not as fooled with my little show as I'd like him to be.

"Heavy flow. And dark chocolate."

"You got her?"

"Yep," Cole answers from the hallway.

Jayden sighs. For a second, I fear he's going to call me on my bullshit. But he doesn't. He stalks out of the room. A few minutes later, the alarm chimes on the front door. I hear the low rumble of the men's voices briefly before Jayden leaves.

I wait. My plan hinges on Cole coming in to chain me to my bed. I wait and wait and wait till despair starts to creep in. He's not going to. He won't come in time. Jayden will come back before I can get away.

But, what feels like forever later, he comes in. I'm lying under the covers and stir as if he woke me, gripping the glass spice container.

"Shhh, back to sleep, little one." He bends down to pick the cuff off the floor.

I strike, whipping the covers back and slamming my weapon into the back of his head.

He crumples and falls to the floor, unmoving. I stare at his large form. For a second, I feel bad.

No. I scramble to put the cuff on him, then pat him down for his knife.

Fuck! He doesn't have it. I check again, panic rolling through me. I can't believe that worked. I look around the room and then throw on my extra clothes.

Cole still lies motionless. I pause. He's still breathing. I take his shoes and socks off too. I put the socks on myself and take the shoes with me.

I do a quick search of the living room. There! His knife is sitting by a half-whittled horse. I grab it and sprint to the door.

This is when my countdown really begins. I don't know the code for the alarm. Jayden is going to know as soon as I get out that door.

I take a deep breath and run outside.

# COLE

## 13

I GROAN. PAIN LANCES MY SKULL, MAKING LIGHT DANCE behind my eyelids. There's an alarm blaring.

Fuck. I pry my eyes open and don't recognize where I am. There's a wood floor and a bed above me.

The cabin. Jayden. The girl.

The girl! I rise to my hands and knees, groaning. She knocked me the fuck out.

As I stand, I hear a clank. I look down to see my wrist cuffed. For a second, I flash back to when I was a child, chained up and alone, except for when I wasn't.

I press my free hand to my eyes and force myself back to reality. I bark out a laugh. That damn minx.

Jayden's gonna be pissed.

I fish in my pocket for the small key that my past forces me to always keep on me.

There's a blaring noise that shoots pain through my head. I realize the door alarm is going off. I also hear my phone ringing in the distance.

I start moving that way and realize I'm barefoot. She's taken my shoes and socks.

I grin as I pick up my phone. Jayden's voice bites, "What's going on?"

"It would appear our little prey has managed to escape for the moment."

There's a deadly silence.

I head to the door to turn off the alarm. "Don't freak out, brother, we'll get her."

"Fuck," he growls. "I've been calling you for five minutes."

"I was indisposed for a bit. She knocked me over the head."

"Christ, I knew something was up. I shouldn't have left."

"Where are you?"

"On my way back. Maybe 20 minutes out."

I head downstairs for shoes, keeping Jayden on the line. I picture running her down. Grabbing her little body and pinning her beneath me. Her cry of fear. Her useless scrambles to get away.

I grin. My dick is hard as stone.

There's plastic rustling on the other end of the line. "Fucking goddamn *chocolate*."

I huff out a laugh. "We disconnected that fuse on my car; she's not going anywhere."

A thrill runs through me. Oh she's going to be fun to hunt.

## 14

COLE IS WAITING FOR ME ON THE FRONT PORCH WHEN I burn up in my truck. He rests his forearms on his knees, appearing relaxed. I know he isn't. He's itching for the chase.

I get out and slam the door, locking it in case she's lurking somewhere close. My breath puffs in the night air.

Cole stretches.

"You didn't move any of the guns, did you?"

"No, they're still in my closet. She doesn't have access."

"She has my knife."

"That must be what she cut the tracker off with." I got a notification shortly after the door alarm that she had cut it off. It stopped tracking her near the garage.

"I hope she uses it." His eyes glint. He looks dark. Like he did all those years ago.

I'm angry. Angry at her for slipping through our fingers. Angry at her for lying to us.

Angry at myself for falling for it. Clearly, I hadn't been heavy enough with her.

I throw on some winter gear and grab a flashlight. Despite myself, I wonder how her feet are doing in this cold. The thought angers me. How dare she be so *stupid*? I grab a vial of the concoction I gave her when I first took her and a syringe.

The closest neighbors are five miles off. She's had around a 40-minute head start. With no shoes, no flashlight, and injured, there's no way she's made it that far. She's just going to get herself hurt.

Cole is waiting for me downstairs. He has a nasty bump on the back of his head.

"What did she get you with?"

"Onion powder." He throws a spice jar into the air and catches it again.

I look at him. "The champion wrestler, 15 years of experience, taken down by a small woman and seasoning?"

He flashes his teeth in a feral grin. "I think I'm in love."

"Well then, lover boy. Let's go get our girl."

I lock the house up before we leave. One less place for her to hide. We start at the garage, scouring it thoroughly. She's not there.

Cole spent much of his high school years hunting in these woods, so I let him take the lead once we were done with the garage. We go to the East, in the opposite direction of the abandoned house on the property. Cole immediately starts into the dark woods, like he's seeing a blazing trail. I don't see anything, but I trust his experience. I won't ruin our night vision by keeping the flashlight on. The moon is out, and its light filters through the barren tree branches well enough to cast shadows. We move quickly, generally following a pattern down the hills. Down is also the way to town. In hilly areas, towns are often situated in valleys because that put them next to the waterways back in the day. Clever girl.

Cole starts to speed up. We jog, our longer legs undoubtedly eating up more space than hers could, until we reach a stream. The moonlight bounces off it, making it look silver.

I say, "There's no way her feet have held up this long."

"Well, when you're running from two devilishly handsome men," he throws me a smirk, "who make you question everything in your safe, boring life, I think you'd be surprised." He's walking up and down the bank. "She must have walked the stream a bit."

"She's going to get frostbite."

I follow him upstream for a bit until he gives a grunt of triumph. "Got her. She's getting tired." He points at the half-frozen ground. "Slipped right here."

"Hurry," I growl at him.

We pick up the pace. Cole points out places she's getting sloppy. Broken branches and slip marks in piles of leaves. We are getting close. It makes my adrenaline spike.

By a large boulder, Cole motions for me to be quiet. We're up a hill and can see down into a small gully. The area is covered with tall, sparse trees and patches of dead undergrowth. A small stream runs downhill.

There! A flash of movement and blond hair. She's close.

I smile. It's time to play, little kitten.

# Mary Jo

## 15

THE DARKNESS CREEPS ME THE FUCK OUT. THE MOON'S shadows hide so many alcoves, overhangs, and brushy areas. Perfect for wildlife—or people—to hide in. I keep thinking about coyotes and bears, and every time I see a big shadow, I think the gig is up. I almost wish the moon wasn't out.

I trip on another stick. Cole's socks are soaked, and my feet are numb. His shoes didn't fit and were only going to slow me down. The rest of me is staying pretty warm, and I wonder for the hundredth time how long I've been out here. I plan what I'm going to say when I find a road. Help, two men kidnapped me and have been holding me hostage in their cabin. Description? Tall. Tattooed. Hot, really hot. Fuck. I'm fucked up.

A stick cracks on the hill to my left. I snap my head that way and freeze. I don't see any movement in the night. My heart hasn't stopped racing since I cut the monitor off.

It was nothing. A squirrel. I slow my breathing and keep going.

A voice sing-songs, "Kiiiiiitteeeeeeen." It's deep and close as fuck.

A scream rips through me, and I take off. Terror burns

through my veins. Holy shit, how did they find me? I've never been more scared in my life.

"Someone's been a bad girl." It's the same voice, Jayden, on my left. I veer to my right. Where's Cole?

I reach the end of the gully, and there, in a small clearing, stands a shadowed, hulking form. I scream again. The sound is loud in the crisp air. I skid to my right, turning to go back the way I came. Fuck, fuck, fuck. I scramble for Cole's knife in my pocket.

A hard body slams into me, and I'm snatched up into the air.

"Oh, kitten," Jayden's voice purrs in my ear. "You shouldn't have run."

I get the knife in my right hand. Cole appears in front of me, then the world blurs, and I'm pressed up against a tree. Strong arms wrestle to get mine. I slash with the knife.

"Shit, watch her."

An iron grip locks around my wrist and cranks. I cry out, pain blazing through me. I realize I've dropped the knife. Fuck! My arms are yanked behind my back, and I'm solidly pinned.

I scream again. Cole groans beside me. "Stop that, little one. I'm going to come in my pants, and we haven't even started."

"Let me go! Fuck you! Help! Someone help!"

Jayden leans what feels like his whole body weight into me.

Cole flips the knife. "I didn't know you liked knife play, little one. Kinky."

I keep fighting, bucking, and squirming against the tree. "Let me go, you sick bastards."

Jayden groans.

Cole leans close to me. "Were you going to use this on me? Cut me with my own knife?"

"Yes," I hiss.

"Hmmm." He rubs the flat of the blade against my cheek. I jerk my face away, scraping it on the tree's rough bark.

"What were you going to do after that? Lick my blood off it? Fuck yourself with it?"

"What?" I tremble.

"What a nasty little girl."

Jayden buries his face in my hair and pulls in a deep breath. I feel his chest expanding from where he's pressed into me.

"Watch out, Jay."

Jayden shifts slightly, and a cold blade presses to my right hip. I stop breathing.

"Let me help you with these." There's a ripping noise, and he cuts all the way down my pant leg. He does the same with every layer I have on until the scraps are hanging down and cold air rushes up my leg and to my wet core.

Jayden eases up on the pressure so I can shift slightly to see Cole better. He looks violent. He pulls something out of his pocket. It shines dull in the moonlight. The spice shaker.

My heaving breathing stills. I feel the rough bark under me. The pressure of Jayden's fingers. His steady rise and fall of breath. I feel my heart beat fast, like a rabbit.

"I'm all for being fair." Cole reaches out and caresses my bare thigh. "You fucked me with this, so I'll fuck you with it."

I gasp.

He spits on it, and I feel his hand go between our legs and up to my center.

I start fighting for real now. Jayden presses me into the tree, my struggles barely moving him.

"No, no, no, no!"

"Fuck." He looks up at Jayden with dark eyes. "She's so wet."

I bury my nose in the tree, embarrassed he can tell how turned on I am.

Jayden's chest rumbles. "Relax, kitten. Let him in."

Cole's fingers massage my clit, spreading the wetness around until the cool air hits it, and I'm struck with both heat and cold. He pushes a finger into me. I gasp and still.

"You feel me in you? This is my pussy. His pussy. It can be as depraved as you want, but only for us."

I feel his arm flexing between our legs, and he puts another finger in. He pumps them in and out while playing with my clit with his thumb. Wet sucking sounds fill the night.

"Goddamn, Cole," Jayden says.

I tremble in Jayden's hold. "Fuck...you." But my voice is breathy. Cole chuckles, and I buck.

"So responsive," he says. He works me expertly, and I fight pleasure. I feel Jayden's hardness press into my lower back. I'm no longer fighting him. I'm fighting myself. Not to feel this. Not to enjoy it. I think about home. I think about Kyle.

Cole slaps my pussy, hard. "Where did you go, little one? Get out of your head."

Despite myself, I moan. The pain was shooting, and the pleasure immediately after just as much so. It made my knees buckle a little. Jayden holds me up.

Cole smacks me again, and I cry out this time. He pinches my clit between his fingers and pulls it away from my body rhythmically, in a pulsing motion. "That's right. Hate me. Hate me so damn good."

My entire body stiffens.

"Yes, kitten," Jayden murmurs in my ear. "Come for him."

I can't help it. Lightning shoots through me, and I come hard. I pulse and pulse, breathing hard and ragged.

I don't notice Cole move. Suddenly there's something cold and hard against my pussy.

"Relax."

I stiffen.

"It's not that big. Our cocks are bigger, you better get used to it."

"Please..." I squirm to get away. To relieve the overstimulation.

"Please, what, little one? Please make it good? Please don't make it hurt?" His voice lowers, "Oh, but I think you like a little pain with your pleasure."

He presses the shaker slightly into me, and I cry out. My pussy stretches to get around it. The unforgiving edges burn.

"Good girl. You're doing so good." He pushes it in more.

I press back against Jayden to get away. Cole adds a finger to my clit, and the already sensitive area quickly responds. The pain mixes with pleasure.

"Cole," I breathe.

"Mhmm?" I feel his arm moving gently up and down and the hard object inside as he fucks me.

I groan, "I can't..."

Jayden shushes me, "You don't have to do anything. Just take it."

I drop my head against the tree. I want to fight the pleasure again. At that moment, Jayden leans in and bites my neck hard, and Cole pushes the bottle deep inside while pressing on my clit. I come. I give a shuddering cry, a mix of tears, pain, and pleasure.

The world blurs a bit as I come down. I breathe and barely notice Jayden shifting behind me. He brushes his nose to my neck, making me shiver and bare it for him.

Sharp pain bites into my neck and stings. I jerk.

"Easy. We've got you."

"What—"

"I'm getting déjà vu," Jayden purrs into my ear. "Last time we did this, you became mine."

Oh shit. Did he drug me? I struggle, but he has me in an iron hold. I kick and fight until the world blurs and spins. Until I can't anymore.

∽

Everything feels fuzzy, like my brain is wrapped in cotton candy. Something buzzes.

I moan. I hear familiar voices in the background. Deep, guttural voices.

Some of the fog clears.

"...waking up..."

The buzzing continues, as does vibrating right above my ass.

I try to open my eyes, but light filters in, and I squint. I see colors and shapes that look slightly off, like I'm looking at the world through a bubble.

I moan.

"Relax, kitten."

Jayden.

I do relax. But something tells me I shouldn't. Why?

The vibrating turns to a buzzing, which turns to tiny pinpricks.

I shift, trying to ease the feeling, but I hardly move anywhere. I realize there's a weight on the back of my legs.

No, not a weight. A body.

A sick feeling overwhelms me. I rub my eyes and do my best to open them again. I see I'm on the couch in the cabin. It's morning, and the sun is blinding me. Cool air brushes my back. The pinpricks are becoming more painful.

I twist my neck around. Jayden is sitting on the back of my legs, holding a tattoo gun. He flashes me a smug smile. His eyes are cold.

Fuck, Jayden! My escape. The memories flash through me.

I start to fight.

"Stop. You don't want to ruin the pretty piece I'm putting on you." The pinpricks pause. I freeze. They start again.

Is he...tattooing me?

I push to get up.

Cole's voice comes, sounding bored. "Stop, little one. He'll put you back out. He's kind of a perfectionist when it comes to his art."

"What the hell?" I stop moving. "I don't want a tattoo!"

"Should have thought of that when you ran."

I crane my neck to see what he's doing.

"Lay down; you can see it when I'm done."

"Are you giving me a *tramp stamp?*"

He chuckles. There's no mirth in it.

A wave of rage flows through me. I barely check it. I don't want him to drug me again, and I know he will. Rage is followed by frustration, followed by crippling sadness.

I turn my face into the couch to hide my emotions. I failed. I tried to get away, and I'm back here *again*.

Nausea slams into me.

"I think I'm going to be sick." I barely lean over the couch's edge before I'm vomiting onto the floor.

Soon a trash can is put under me. I heave into it until I'm dry heaving. And I keep going. I puke nothing until tears stream down my face.

Finally, the waves of nausea end. I hang my head on the edge of the trash can and heave in a breath.

I realize someone is holding my hair back. I look up. Cole looks concerned.

"I think you gave her too much."

"I didn't give her any more than last time."

I close my eyes and lay my head back down. I remember the chase. The intoxicating fear when they hunted me down. The lust when they took me; when they made me come. My pussy gets wet again, and I scrunch my eyes shut.

"Kitten." Jayden has stopped tattooing me.

Slowly, I move my eyes back to him.

His gaze is shuttered. "Are you going to be sick again?"

I take stock of how I feel. Like shit, but not like throwing up.

"No," I mutter. Arrogant fucker. Inconvenienced by my puking when he forced the drugs on me. Or maybe mad at me for running. I don't care. Either way, he asked for it.

He gets back to tattooing me. When he's done, he gets off me. My back feels like it's on fire. I stand and stretch, glaring at both men, hoping it makes me look hard. Inside, though, I feel...tired.

I cross my arms. Jayden pulls out his phone and snaps a picture, flipping it around so I can see.

He's tattooed both of their names between the two dimples in my back. I gasp.

Cole makes an appreciative sound. "Goddamn. It's so hot to have you branded as ours."

I want to say something, but no words come out. It's clear Jayden has skill, and the names are written in clean, legible, flowy script, though my skin is raised in irritation. Jayden starts to tend to it.

"I hate it," I say in monotone.

"Wash and lotion it twice a day, and don't scratch it."

I wait for the anger in me. It doesn't come. "Can I go to bed?"

Both of them give me quick looks as if that wasn't the reaction they were expecting.

"Have anything else tucked in there to hit me with?" Cole asks.

"No."

He shrugs. I start to go to my room, but Jayden says, "Crawl, kitten."

I snap to look at him.

"Remember the rules. You break a rule, you crawl."

I hate it. I hate him. I hate everything. But I drop to my knees and crawl to my room. I feel their heated stares on my ass as I leave. When I get to my room, I shut the door almost all the way. I vaguely notice there are warm, fuzzy socks on my feet. I drop on my stomach on the bed and close my eyes. What the hell were they thinking? Tattoos are fucking permanent. How am I going to explain this to Kyle?

Fuck. I just need sleep. Just sleep, and I'll figure out a way to get home after that.

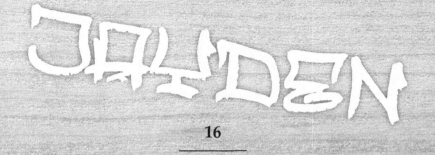

## 16

MY BEDROOM DOOR CLICKS SHUT, AND I'M STARTLED AWAKE.

Instantly, I know. Dread starts in my belly and moves out.

The bed dips, and I squeeze my eyes shut. I've stopped believing that closing my eyes will make it stop, but I do it anyway.

# COLE

## 17

"GET UP." OUR GIRL HAS BEEN IN HER ROOM FOR TWO DAYS. She only comes out to eat; otherwise, she stares at the wall. I'm worried about her.

She looks at me from her bed. Her blue eyes are vibrant, looking vulnerable and angry even in the soft light. She's a strong woman, but I've been watching her get beat down. I tried to tell Jayden he can't go so fast with her or he'll break her mind too far. But as usual, he doesn't listen.

There's an art to shattering someone without driving them insane. Sometimes, you have to break them gently, kindly even. Then, you can build them back up slowly in the direction you want them to go.

"I'm tired." She turns away.

"Too bad, lemon drop." I pull the blanket off her. "You're joining me downstairs. I'm going to teach you how to whittle."

She's in nothing but a tank top and some thin black panties, and she snatches the sheet to try and cover herself. My dick immediately hardens. I flash back to how wet her pussy got for me, the sounds she made, the sweet victory of catching her. I nearly groan.

She glares at me and hops out of bed, snatching a pair of sweatpants on the chair.

"You're gambling a lot that I won't cut your balls off and stuff them down your throat and up your ass."

I grin at her. "I'd love to see you try. It's hot when you get violent like that." I turn to go downstairs. "Come."

I hear her pause, probably deciding if she's going to obey. It brings another grin to my face. She makes a decision because I hear her follow.

I flip on the lights in my old room. She stills, just outside my doorway. My room has a desk, an old twin bed opposite the door, and a bean bag from when I was a teen. There are old posters on the wood-paneled walls. I grab my old shoebox of items and sit on the bed.

She eyes me warily. I pat the bed beside me. "I don't bite. That's all Jayden."

She crosses her arms while I get out my supplies. I rummage through a bunch of figures that I've carved over the years. There are only a few of the pieces I've made in here. Most end up in the fire when I'm done because what am I going to do with them? I've gotten better as time goes on, getting the small details refined. There's something therapeutic for me in keeping my hands busy with my knife. I grab a small wood scrap that hasn't been used.

"Here." I flip my knife out of my pocket and hold it out. It's the pearl-handled one she took from me. The one I usually use. My mom gave it to me when I was a kid. She probably stole it from someone, but I've kept it all the same.

She takes it and then sits on the bean bag, as far away from me as she can get. I toss her a scrap of wood.

"What kinds of things do you like?"

"What?" she asks.

"What do you like?" I get another knife from the box and grab a scrap for myself. "I think of things I like, and they just emerge for me. Mostly horses, sometimes other animals, houses, people."

"Horses?"

"Yeah. Always liked them."

She's showing no interest in starting yet, so I get to work on my own piece. She's silent for a while until she asks, "Did you ever have one?"

"What, a horse? Nah." I shave the pieces right onto the floor. I'll sweep them up later. "We were white trash. Hardly money for my mom's habit, let alone food," I chuckle.

When she doesn't make a sound, I look up. Fuck. I forgot some people don't have a sense of humor about that kind of stuff. She stares, then drops her head and mutters something.

"What?"

She clears her throat, "Food."

I raise an eyebrow.

"What I like. Food."

I smile and point at her block of wood. "Exactly, food." I start explaining the basics of carving, going over things I've learned over the years. She watches quietly. A few times I can tell she's thinking of stabbing me, and it makes my dick hard. But she keeps quiet and to herself, and soon starts on her block.

I watch her use my knife out of the corner of my eye. I think about how I used that knife to cut her pants off. My dick is so hard it's painful. I've beat myself off to that memory many times. I want to use it to cut her skin. Watch the pretty red blood bead up against her pale skin.

We work in loaded silence, the snick and scrape of the knives the only sounds.

I break the silence. "You know, Sage was obsessed with you when they were together."

I feel her gaze snap to me. "Who?"

I ignore her. "She'd watch all your videos and make your recipes, talking his ear off about you."

She digests that information. I can almost hear her brain churning.

"Why does he hate me?"

"He doesn't hate you."

She laughs. The sound is husky and beautiful. "Yes, he does."

I shrug. "Okay."

We work in silence again for a long time. I occasionally help her with little questions. She's making a bowl of ice cream. Finally, I hear her stomach grumble.

I hold out my hand for the knife. She seems hesitant. Like it's a life jacket, and she's drowning in the ocean.

"My mom gave it to me," I say.

She looks at me. I don't tell her that it's cut the lips, eyelids, foreskin, and asshole off a man before. I wanted a dull knife to draw out his agony. Like he did for me.

She hands it back silently. I put it back on my desk and make sure she hasn't swiped anything else. The beautiful little thief. Before I take her back upstairs, I put my project back into the shoebox. It's looking an awful lot like the little blond woman who has stormed into our lives.

# Mary Jo

## 18

Jayden stands over my bed. "Time to get up. We're going out."

"What?" I rub my eyes.

"Get a jacket. It's cold out." His voice is cold. Colder than normal.

I sit up. The room is dark. Did he say we were going out? I was going out?

I scramble to my feet and grab a jacket. Jayden is already out in the kitchen.

"Where are we going?"

He looks at me but doesn't say anything. Cole comes up from the basement. He also seems unusually sober.

Dread pools in my stomach. What is going on? I take a step back.

"Now, now." Jayden glares at me. "You wanted to leave so bad. Now you're going to. Let's go." He motions at the front door.

I look at Cole.

He lifts an eyebrow. "You gonna obey, little one?"

I look back at Jayden and notice something in his waistband. A gun.

Adrenaline fills me, and I take a small step back. "You going to shoot me?"

Jayden cuts his gaze to me. He looks lethal. "Go."

I don't want to. Every instinct is screaming at me not to go. But somehow, I do.

We walk out to the truck in silence. My thoughts are going a thousand miles an hour. I pushed it too far yesterday. Would he tell me to get a jacket if he was just going to kill me? Why am I not running right now?

Cole must sense my indecision. He grabs my arm and tucks me into him. With horror, I realize he also has a gun tucked into his waistband. He keeps my arm pinned to him and away from it. We get to the truck, and he opens the back door, pushing me in. Jayden jumps in on the other side. Cole goes to the driver's side and gets in, starting the car.

"These are the rules: you sit there like a good girl and be quiet. It's pretty simple. Do you understand?"

I look down at his waistband. I nod.

Jayden moves his right hand to his pocket, and I jump. He pulls out a cloth and turns to me. "Blindfold."

"No." It slips out before I can stop it. No. I want to see before he shoots me in the head. I need to see it.

"Little one," Cole growls in warning from the front.

Jayden's eyes are hard. If he was going to kill me, why would he care if I saw where we went? But who knows with these psychopaths.

When I don't move, Jayden puts it on me, and my world goes dark. I start to panic again. I'm completely at their mercy.

Cole starts the car, and I lurch as we begin to move. What purpose could they have to move me? Maybe we were moving locations. Maybe the police were hot on their tail. That thought fills me with brief joy, but they didn't pack anything. Maybe they weren't going to kill me. Why go through the trouble of marking me as theirs and then killing me off?

Oh fuck. The tattoo could be their calling card. They could be serial murderers. It strikes me how little I actually know about these men.

My breathing is heavy. A hand drops on my knee, and I jump. He keeps it there, heavy and warm.

We drive for what feels like hours. At first, it feels like hills and twists and turns, and it makes me feel sick. Then it flattens out, and we just drive and drive. I need to pee, but I don't dare ask them. Jayden keeps his hand on my knee the whole time. The touch grounds me. I can do this. I may not survive, but I'll kill them before I give up.

Finally, the car stops. Cole gets out, and my door opens with a rush of cold wind.

"Scoot over." He pushes in next to me. Jayden then gets out his side.

Cole takes my blindfold off. It's still dark out. We're parked in what looks to be a parking lot. Of a church, maybe? Jayden is walking across the lot, hands shoved in his pockets.

"Where are we?"

"That's not relevant to you, little one."

I turn to look at him. He has an edge to him today that he doesn't normally have. My gut sinks. We sit in silence. My tattoo itches.

"I need to pee."

"Hold it."

"What's going on?"

"You'll find out soon enough."

I'm moving from scared to pissed off. "You know what? No. You don't get to drag me out here and then not answer anything. Tell me what's going on."

Cole leans into my space, his toned body suddenly feeling

bigger and more menacing than before. "Do you think I won't hurt you? I will. And I'll enjoy it. Stop pushing your luck."

My heart races. He hasn't raised his voice, but it felt like his voice filled the car.

"Do not push Jayden." He sits back. "Not today."

# JAYDEN

## 19

Sage has moved. Thinking I won't find her. Thinking it makes her safe. It's laughable really.

I know that making someone disappear is about careful thinking, planning, and luck. Luck that the neighbors won't be up and look outside. That they won't call the cops. That if they do call the cops, that there won't be officers in the area for a fast response. I know because I lived on the other side of it.

Sage has a camera on her front door, so I avoid it. Before we left, I smudged my license plates with mud. I left Cole and my kitten parked about a block away and walk through the neightbor's side and backyards. The ground is still frozen, so I won't leave any footprints. I'll still throw these shoes away, just in case.

The light is on in Sage's double. I hang by the neighbor's shed. Her backyard isn't big, maybe 75 feet, but there aren't any trees or anything to provide cover. Her habit is to let her dog out at five. It was one of her biggest gripes about her lab, Harriet—she was as needy as a baby.

I wait. Five rolls around. Then five-ten. I glance at my watch again. My thoughts keep going back to my kitten. The fear she had today was unbearably hot. Intoxicating. Made me want to delay my plans just to fuck her in the backseat. It took monumental effort not to do so.

Finally, Sage opens the sliding door, and Harriet runs out. She shuts it again. She looks the same. She's still tall, brunette, and slim.

I walk to the side of her house. Harriet greets me, sniffing at me and spinning in excited circles. I pat her head and get down to her level, grabbing her collar. I wait around the corner of the house, just out of sight. Harriet licks my hand repeatedly.

Sage waits a few minutes before I hear the door open again. "Harriet!"

She doesn't come because I don't let her.

We wait. There's a frustrated huff, and she calls again. Harriet whines.

"For Christ's sake dog." I hear the door open a little more, and Sage steps out.

I have my gun in her ribs before she can get two feet out the door. I grip the side of her neck and hiss, "Not a word."

She stiffens.

"Thought you could hide from me?"

"Jayden," she breathes. She starts to tremble.

"Say goodbye to Harriet."

"Fuck you." But she's shaking, and her voice cracks.

Her hatred doesn't turn me on. It burns like acid in my stomach. I shake her hard. "Fucking walk."

I yank her around and open the sliding door with my hand not holding the gun. Harriet darts inside, away from the cold. I use my other hand to pat Sage down quickly. She is in thin pajamas. No phone.

"You're a psychopath, Jayden. When I don't show up to work, they'll call the police."

I don't honor her with an answer and push her back the way I came. She's stiff and resistant. I dig my gun into the thin skin over her ribs. As we get through the neighbor's yard and can see the church, she starts looking around. Her fists start clenching, and her breathing gets heavy. She's going to run. Or scream.

I slam the butt of my gun into her head. She crumples.

Fuck. It's a lot more suspicious to carry someone to a car than walk them there. This fucking bitch. I throw her over my shoulder and shoot a text.

COLE AND I SIT IN SILENCE. THE CAR IS STILL RUNNING.

Cole's phone dings. He crawls across me into the front seat and puts the car in drive.

I think about jumping out of the car, but it's only a brief thought. Not with a gun in play. We drive into a neighborhood right by the church. There's a shadow on the sidewalk. It gets close, and I see it's Jayden. Carrying something over his shoulder.

A person.

I gasp.

Jayden wrenches the back passenger door open and tosses the person in. It's a woman. She flops to the seat, head by my waist. There's blood everywhere.

Holy shit. I can't take my eyes off her. She appears unconscious. Or she's dead. I'm torn away from looking at her by my door opening and a rush of cold air coming in. I scream.

Jayden jumps over me and sits between me and the girl. "Drive Cole."

The truck lurches, and we go the normal speed down the

road. Instead of thinking about anything important, I think about how Jayden must be getting blood on his jeans.

I'm sucking in deep breaths. The girl's head moves with the car, and I see her face.

Ice shoots through my veins.

She's familiar. Where have I seen this girl before? Why do I know her?

She moans. Jayden pulls his gun out and lays it across his legs, pointing at the girl.

I don't ask anything. He looks at me, does a double take, and yanks the blindfold back up over my eyes. I feel him lean into me. "Have you enjoyed your time, kitten?"

"No," I murmur and tremble. He just kidnapped another woman. Cole helped. She might be dead. These men are crazy. I need to get away. They're going to kill me. Us.

Jayden leans in and takes a deep breath. Is he...smelling me?

I scoot back until I'm pressed into the car door. He follows, and his weight moves on top of me.

"No!" My heart is pounding. Racing. I need to get away. I push him away and scramble for my blindfold and the door handle.

"You should know better than to try and escape me," he growls in my ear. He yanks my pants down.

I yank down my blindfold and rush to get them back up. His mouth is on my clit before I can, hot and wet. He reaches up to grab my breast and pinches my nipple so hard I scream.

I grip his hair with both hands and yank him away from me as hard as I can. He groans and pushes back into me harder, eating me with enthusiasm. I scratch and claw, but he only pins my hands to my stomach and continues. There's no room for me to kick him as my right leg is pinned between his body and the front seat, and my left is on the girl. Her warm blood is soaking my sock.

Fuck, the girl.

I struggle, only giving extra friction on my clit. Sensation shoots through me. I pant and growl, but my hands don't move. I can't get away.

"If you think you'll get away, you're mistaken. You're my prize, and I'm going to claim you." He makes eye contact with me and sucks my clit into his mouth, and sucks hard. My body responds, jerking into him. What the hell is wrong with me? I start to cry in frustration. Jayden's eyes bore into me, and he groans.

"Fuck," Cole says from the front seat. His expression is ravenous.

Jayden sucks with more enthusiasm. He makes my body feel good. Too good. It keeps bucking into him for friction. I haven't peed yet, and the pressure adds to the pleasure. The pleasure builds until my orgasm tears through me, and I cry out.

Jayden crawls up over me, and then his dick is in my face. I realize I've never seen it and the car is too dark to see it now. The tip is at my lips.

"Suck," he says in a husky voice. My mind is glazed in pleasure still. I instinctively open, and he pushes into my mouth. He pistons in fast and hard, and I choke right away. He's big. I hollow my cheeks and do my best to breathe as he pounds my face. He's brutal and rough, and I choke and gag, but he doesn't let up.

His pounding gets faster, and he growls, "Swallow."

He stops, and cum shoots down my throat. He's so far in I have no choice but to swallow. He pulses over and over into me so long I start to pull away to breathe. He grips my hair at the back of my head and yanks me off of him. He tucks himself away and puts his forehead to mine. His eyes are angry and dark. "You will never get away from me. Do you hear me? You're mine. There is no escape."

～

WHEN THE TRUCK STOPS, the men make me stay in the back while they drag the girl out. She woke up at some point in the drive but couldn't seem to stay awake, which didn't seem good. After what felt like an hour of driving, they put the blindfold back on. I cried silently for a long time.

It takes them a while to come get me. When they do, I see we're back in the garage at the cabin. The girl is nowhere in sight, but Cole doesn't let me look and grabs my arm, dragging me toward the cabin.

"I can walk." I try pulling my arm away.

He doesn't relent and marches me inside. His lips are drawn in a thin line, and he punches the alarm code into the door. He sees me watching and before I can move, pins me against the door. I let out a gasp of air.

Cole leans in and says in a low voice, "Not today, little one."

"Why?" I whisper.

His gaze roams over my body. "You have blood on you." He licks his lips.

I look down, trying to see myself where he isn't pressed into me. Holy shit, I do. It's all over my pants and even my top. The girl's lifeblood. I want to rip all my clothes off and scrub myself clean.

"Who is she? I know her."

He looks at me, and I see pity in his gaze for a second. Quickly, it's gone. He doesn't answer.

That brief expression takes all the fight out of me.

"Can I shower?" I whisper.

He steps back. "I don't know. You being covered in blood is the hottest thing I've seen since Jayden took you in the car."

Tears well in my eyes. "You're sick."

He nods. "It's a good thing you are, too."

"I'm not," I hiss. "I'm not the one who kidnapped two people and watched while someone was raped."

Cole's eyes darken, and he closes in on my space, pushing me against the door again. "Did you not enjoy it? Do you not get off on being taken and forced? Did you not enjoy every other time we've touched you? Chased you? Made you come?"

I hate the feeling in my chest. There's pressure like a band around me. Because I did like it. I've come harder and more often than I ever have before. I narrow my eyes in hatred. "That doesn't make it right."

He gives a mocking smile and growls. "Right? Are you saying your fantasies are wrong? Then you're in a shitty place to start judging something you know nothing about."

He grabs my arm and yanks me down to the bathroom. "Shower."

I do. I stay as long as I dare. Until the water has run cold. Until Cole tells me that Jayden needs to get in. That gets me out quick. No matter how hard I try, I can't stop thinking about everything that has happened to me. About the girl. How I knew her. Why Jayden seemed to know me so well before he took me. About my traitorous body.

I vow to never let them make me come again. I've just been weak. It's time I start being strong. It's time to get away from these psychopaths before I end up like *her*.

⁓

JAYDEN CUFFS me to my bed again that night. I can't sleep. My tattoo itches incessantly. I can't help thinking about that girl. I have a feeling she's in the garage. With no heat. Having lost all that blood.

I sit up with a start. The paperclip! I fumble to search under the mattress. It's still there. Frantically, I work it in the keyhole. Soon, my fingers get sweaty, and keeping my grip on it is hard. It takes what feels like forever, but the cuff opens.

I could cry from relief. I put it back under the mattress, grab my sweater from the chair, and sneak to the door. I open it and cringe, although the sound it makes is soft.

The cabin is dark and quiet. I grab some granola bars from the counter and a water bottle. Cole doesn't realize I saw the code to the door. I punch it in and hold my breath. Green lights up the monitor. I pad out the door and shut it softly. Then I'm running to the garage.

It's unlocked again. The cocky motherfuckers. It scares me too. We really must not be close to anything if they feel comfortable leaving things unlocked. I step inside and close the door again.

It's dark. I think about turning the light on, but I don't. I notice the car keys are not hanging where they normally do. So not too cocky, then.

There's what appears to be a small office area to the right, by the stairs. I move to it and open the door.

Beyond a desk is the girl, handcuffed to a metal chair. I gasp.

Her head jerks up. Her hair is matted with blood, but it appears brunette. She has dark circles under her eyes, but she's still gorgeous with tan skin and pretty eyes. She has the body of a supermodel.

I rush over to her. "Are you okay?"

She blinks at me. Of course, she isn't.

Her voice comes out raspy, "Water?"

"Fuck. Yes." I grab the bottle from my pocket and try to hand it to her, but realize her hands are bound. I snap the seal and hold it to her mouth.

She drinks in long pulls. She doesn't stop until it's all gone then eyes me warily. "He let you see me?"

"Uh, no. I picked the lock."

She looks at me like I have two heads. I see now there's a swollen lump on the side of her head where there's the most blood. She's in penguin pajamas. She must have a concussion.

"What's your name?" I ask her.

"He didn't tell you?" She coughs. "Can you get me out of these?"

Shit. "I left the paperclip in the cabin."

"Paperclip?" She eyes me again.

"Yeah, I stole it from Cole..." I look her over again. "What's going on? Why did they take you?"

Deep, animalistic fear comes across her face. In a quiet voice, she says, "He's going to hurt me."

The words drop ice in my belly. He wouldn't...would he? I swallow. Yes, he would.

I see goosebumps prickle across her skin. I shrug out of my sweater. "Here." I try to figure out how to put it on her without the arms. I settle on pulling it over her body and the back of the chair.

"Thanks," she mutters.

"I have food." I pull out the granola bars. She doesn't seem interested, but I break off little pieces, and when I offer them to her, she eats them. We sit in silence for a while with just the sounds of her eating. Something rustles in the garage. I jump and look over my shoulder. It's a barn cat.

"How did you meet Jayden?" she finally asks.

"He kidnapped me," I say.

She looks at me. "You're not together?"

I take a step back, horrified. "What? No!"

She doesn't look convinced. She leans her head back and closes her eyes. "I'm not sure why he sent you out here, but I'm tired. Thanks for the food."

"How do you know Jayden? Who are you?"

She cracks her eyes open, looking annoyed. "I'm Sage. His ex?"

I stand, stunned. It feels like the world stops spinning, and the only things that exist are her, me, and this room. His ex? Jayden has an ex? Of course he does. I look over her gorgeous form and feel anger trickle through me.

A deep laugh startles both of us, and I whip around.

Jayden is standing in the doorway, hands up against the doorframe, leaning into it. The hairs on the back of my neck prickle.

"Kitten, what are you doing out here?"

I move to step back but freeze when his eyes narrow on me like a predator. "Let's get you back inside. It's cold out here."

"Fuck you. You can't keep her out here like an animal."

He looks bored and pushes off the doorframe. "This is your only warning. Let's go, or I'll make sure she misses her next feeding."

My mouth drops open. He waits expectantly. When his eyebrow quirks up, I jump and scramble over.

"Good girl." He grabs my wrist. "Say goodnight, kitten."

"Fuck you," I mutter again.

He gives a sharp jerk that yanks me to him. I slam into his chest and look up. Before I can react, he grips my chin and pulls me in for a kiss. It's harsh and claiming. He pulls me out into the main garage and shuts the office door before I yank my mouth away.

"Let her go! She didn't do anything. You can't just take people and say they're yours!" I pry at the fingers holding my wrist. They don't budge. "We're people, damn it. Let go of me."

He doesn't say anything, just pulls me toward the cabin. Panic mounts in me. My heart is pounding, and I claw at his hand now.

"Fuck you, fuck you," I chant. "Let me go."

We get through the front door, and I launch myself at his eyes.

"Jesus." He jerks his head back and wraps his arms around me. One of my arms is pinned up by his head, and I grab at anything I can get. Hair, skin. Everything in me tells me to get away from him. That I won't survive if I stay with him. That he'll suck the soul out of me and make me smile while he does it.

"Let me go!"

Jayden wrestles us to the couch, where he drops us down, him on top of me. He tucks his head into my arm so that I no longer have any space to swing at him. I grunt and struggle, but he's heavy. He's touching all over me and weighing me down.

I keep fighting, but he just lays there, holding me. Soon, I'm winded, and I still my movement, panting. My heart races, trying to catch up with my fight. With my need to run. Gradually, it slows. I stop sucking air.

Above me, Jayden starts to relax. His heartbeat is steady against my chest.

"Get off me," I growl. But there's no bite to it.

"No." His fingers start to run through my hair. He's gentle and methodical. He untangles every snarl one by one. I close my eyes so I don't have to look at him.

His weight is a warm pressure that makes my body want to fall asleep. I shake my head to rouse myself. I can't believe I want to fall asleep after what I just saw. He doesn't move; he just keeps combing his fingers down my scalp.

I want to stop feeling what he's making me feel, but I can't move. I fight him and myself for a long time. Soon there are longer and longer periods where I close my eyes, sleep heavy in my limbs.

The last time I startle awake, I glance over the top of the couch to the hallway. I blink once then open them again, sleep making my vision blurry. I think I see Cole standing there, watching us. But then I sleep.

I WAKE FEELING STRANGELY relaxed and rested. I blink and see sunlight streaming into the living room. There's a warmth at my back.

I stiffen. Jayden is lying next to me. We slept here all night. I look around without moving too much. We're still alone.

Fuck. Jayden's breathing is even and soft. He's spooning me with his arm around my middle. I try to lift it off me so I can slip away.

"Lay still, kitten."

I jump. Fuck, he's awake. At first, I'm embarrassed that I fell asleep, but then I get mad. I try to get up again, but he pulls me back into him, tighter than before. Then I feel how hard he is behind me. And how big.

"Stop. Moving," he growls.

"I need to go to the bathroom," I hiss. His arm is a weight against my waist. He nestles his nose into the back of my neck.

"In a minute." He lays there, just breathing me in. Why is this man so comfortable? So dangerous and comfortable at the same time.

Dangerous to more than me. I stiffen.

With a sigh, he finally lets me go. I get up and go to the bathroom, splashing cold water on my face for a long time. I hear Cole's voice, and the two men go back and forth.

When I come back out, I've steeled myself. They're both cooking breakfast; bacon and eggs and...pancakes? My mouth waters.

"You gonna give any of that to Sage?" I cross my arms right outside the kitchen.

"No." Jayden doesn't even look at me. "Scrambled or over easy?"

"I'm not eating shit until you let her eat."

Cole flicks up an eyebrow. He's in a white shirt that makes him look even more tan. He strolls over to me and brushes a hair behind my ear. "Spicy this morning, hmmm, little one? I'll fuck the attitude out of you if you want."

I shove him back. Or, I try. His massive frame doesn't move. "Don't touch me."

He smiles, then grabs the back of my neck. He squeezes hard enough it hurts and leans into me. "Jay asked you a question."

I glare at his blue eyes. "Did you brush your teeth this morning? Nasty."

He crushes his mouth to mine. His lips are bruising, punishing. He bites at my lip hard. I gasp and taste blood. He swoops his tongue into my mouth and licks along the tops of my bottom teeth. I taste spearmint and blood.

"You be the judge." His eyes light with mirth. With the hand on the back of my neck, he shoves me toward the kitchen island. "Eat."

I stiffly sit on the barstool. "I'm not going to, and you can't make me. You starve one of us, you starve us both."

Jayden sets a plate in front of me with bacon, scrambled eggs, and a pile of pancakes drenched in golden syrup. "We can and will make you. You aren't going on a hunger strike for her."

I shove the plate away. "Just what bad thing did she do? Break up with you? As a matter of fact, what bad thing did I do? I've never met you before, and I wish I never had, you evil, kidnapping mother fuck—"

Cole is behind me in a blink. He fists my hair and yanks my head back, laughing in my ear. "God, that smart mouth on you. I love it." He digs his fingers into my jaw, and I cry out from the pain of it. Something moves above me, and Jayden forks food into my mouth. He then clamps his hand over my mouth and pinches my nose.

I can't breathe. I panic, thrashing back and forth, but Cole's hold on my hair is hard and burns.

"Chew, swallow, and you can breathe again."

I feel like I'm choking. I claw my hands at Jayden's arms, earning me an eye-watering tug on my hair.

"Chew. And swallow." Cole's breath is hot in my ear.

I keep fighting, but it gets me nowhere. My lungs burn. Finally, I chew whatever is in my mouth. It's tasteless. I swallow. It's hard to with my neck cranked back.

They immediately let me go. I suck in deep breaths, the air sweet. I look at Jayden, and his pupils are dilated.

"You going to keep doing that for every bite?"

"Fuck. You," I say. But I grab the fork and stab it into some eggs.

"Good girl." Jayden goes back to eating.

I don't have an appetite anymore, but I force myself to eat. The pancakes have a bitter taste to them, and I almost spit them out. "What's in this?"

"No excuses, kitten. They're fine. Eat."

I try another bite, but they taste wrong. "Did you put too much baking powder in?"

"We can go back to feeding you if you like."

"No. I don't 'like'." I glare and force the rest of the food down. "Can I go to my room?"

"No." The men start cleaning up breakfast.

I glare at them, feeling stuffed. They chat on about the weather and how it's supposed to snow tonight.

A wave of dizziness passes through me. I blink.

"Gonna drop to the teens tonight too."

The salt and pepper shakers start to wave, then return to solid again. Jayden stands behind me and wipes the table.

Warmth floods me. What is going on? I try to stand, but it takes a long time for my legs to move. Jayden stays behind me, still talking to Cole.

"I—" My tongue feels fuzzy. I blink. When I open my eyes, I'm slumped over the table. I feel happy. Something tells me I should be upset. I just grin and look at the crumbs on the wood. Pancakes. The pancakes! They put something in my pancakes.

I try to get up, but now my legs really don't work. Cole moves in front of me. Mirth fills me, and I laugh. I have no defenses against them now. I just laugh harder.

## 21

She's feeling the effects of the roofie I put in her syrup. I only put half a dose in, and it'll hit her slower since she ingested it. She's leaning on the table, giggling and scowling.

Cole looks at me, lips tight. "For the record, I think that was kinda a dick move."

I stroke her hair, rolling my eyes. "I am a dick."

"Yeah, but not to her." He crosses his arms.

"Since when?" I scoop her up and move her to the couch.

Cole snorts but doesn't answer. I don't like what he's implying. She's mine, yes. Mine to abuse. Mine to play with. Mine to control. But I don't have feelings for her.

So why is there this nagging...guilt?

I pull out my Shibari ropes. It feels good to touch them all again. To feel their smoothness in my hands. I haven't rigged in years, but from early on, I knew my kitten would be perfect for it. She wants to fight me; I want to make her helpless. She likes to feel afraid and restrained; I like to make her that way, entirely at my mercy.

Cole sits with her on the couch. With her being this relaxed, I'll need his help to hold her into the position I want.

"Let me have her clothes."

Cole starts coaxing her out of her shirt. It slides off her, and there sit her gorgeous tits. They aren't big, but they're perky with tiny, tan nipples. I reach out and stroke one. She moans and tilts her head back.

"Your pants, little one." She starts at Cole's words. I see her open her eyes and try to fight the drug. But Cole slips her pants and panties off as well until she's leaning against his big body, naked. I drink in the sight. She's absolutely stunning. She's small-boned and delicate but every bit a woman. Light hair has grown over her pubic area since I haven't let her have a razor. I know she keeps it shaved when she can. Cole runs his hands up and down her arms.

"Where you putting her?"

"Here." I direct him under the entryway between the living and dining rooms. There are solid exposed beams that run above, supporting the loft area. He drops down to sit with her in his arms. She leans back into him, smiling with half-lidded eyes.

I start with her arms. I wrap them around her torso like she's hugging herself. Like she's trying to protect herself, but it won't work. Her delicate arms are perfect for showcasing the knots. I'm careful to avoid her tattoo. Can't have it blowing out.

She occasionally tries to pull away, but Cole leans over and softly chides her, and she relaxes again. Her mood swings up and down, which is not unusual with the drug I gave her. Occasionally, tears will glisten in her eyes. She'll turn them up at me, and there's no guarded look anymore. Just pure submission. It's the most beautiful thing I've ever seen, but it also aggravates that guilt. I move to her torso, knotting down it in beautiful braids but veering off as I reach her pelvis. I open, bend her legs at the knee, and tie her thigh and calf together like that. I tie them back so she can't close them. It takes a while for me to rig the ropes that will suspend her in the air in the doorway. But I get them just the way I want them, and Cole helps me hoist her up.

And there she hangs. A perfect little toy in a sex swing of my own design. I can do anything I want to her. But no. I won't touch her yet. I have plans. Plans—I remind myself—that have been the only thing keeping me going. Well, until I got my new plaything, Jo.

She keeps nodding off and jerking awake when her head falls forward or back. That's fine. She can sleep off some of the drugs.

Cole and I get to work on the other half of the operation.

# Mary Jo

22

MY HEAD FEELS HEAVY, BUT THE REST OF MY BODY FEELS weightless. Like I'm floating on clouds. At the same time, I feel like I'm wrapped tightly in strong arms.

I open my eyes. The light is bright, and I squint against it. A lamp. A bear lamp on a small table. I look more. A tan couch. I lift my eyes. Sage, sitting in a chair. No, not sitting. Tied to it.

I blink. Some clarity comes back. I'm in the cabin. Why am I on clouds? I look down. I'm suspended off the ground. That can't be right. I try to move, but I can't. I feel like I'm in a dream where I try to run, but my legs won't move.

I blink again. I'm still floating.

"Ah, kitten, you're awake." Jayden's voice fills my head.

I look up at him. He looks enormous and sinful. His chest and arms stretch out his dark T-shirt, which accentuates the dark tattoos on his arms. His gaze is heavy on me.

I lick my lips—at least, I try to. There's something in my mouth. I rear my head back, trying to get it out, but it's still in my mouth.

"What did she take?" I look over. It's Sage.

"*That* shouldn't be what you're worried about." Jayden's voice is dark. I snap my eyes back to him. Why is he angry?

"Fuck you, Jayden. Why don't you just do what you're going to do and let me go."

He laughs. "Oh, Sage." His voice is mocking. "Let you go?"

My mind feels like it's wrapped in translucent film. I see Cole now. He's leaning on the fireplace behind Sage, arms crossed. He's also in a dark T-shirt and cargo pants. Jayden pulls something out of his pocket. It's a phone. He holds it out to her.

Sage looks away. Cole stalks up, grips her hair, and points her head at the screen. It seems like he's playing a video for her. I hear voices, loud music, laughter.

Wait. I scrunch my eyes closed. Why does that sound like me?

"Remember that?" Jayden asks her. He then walks over to me. He holds a phone in front of me. The video is paused, but it looks familiar. There's a club in the background and Sage's face. She's in a little black dress with red lipstick. It's tugging at the fog in my mind. Jayden presses play and heavy music blares.

"Hey, dipshit." Sage's voice comes across. The video pans over to the seat next to her. And there I am. In my sparkly blue club dress. The one I wore for New Year's. With the plum eyeshadow I tried for the first time that day.

Clarity hits me like a smack in the face. New Years. The club in Columbus. Kyle and I went and I drank Tequila like it was water, and then I kissed a girl I met at the bar. Sage. *I kissed Sage.* My eyes snap to Jayden's. His gaze is shuttered.

The video keeps playing. Sage is pointing the camera at me. "Say something to my abusive ex."

Video me smiles, batting her eyelashes slowly. I look beyond the camera and reach over. I pull Sage into me. The video wobbles but catches us fully making out. I kiss her long and deep, and when I pull away, I look at the camera, licking my lips. "Happy New Year, fucking asshole. May you never get laid again." I laugh and lift a shot glass full of clear liquid to the camera, then shoot it down.

The video pans to the bottles of liquor behind the bar and then stops.

I forgot a lot of those details until now. Her little black dress. Her gold eyeshadow. My hair was in a high ponytail. The video. I was so drunk that night. I do remember Kyle cried for a long time because even though he told me to kiss a girl on New Year, that it would be hot, he thought Sage was too hot.

I open my mouth to say something, but I can't speak. I realize there's a gag in it. I look around again. The fog clears slightly, and I see that my legs are tied and I'm...naked. Panic rolls through me, but the film follows close behind, and the fear backs off. It just hovers in the corners of the room.

Jayden turns back to Sage. "You found out I still had my mom's phone, and you sent it to that because I blocked you."

Sage whimpers.

"I want you to watch this, Sage." His voice is dark. "And I want you to think about why I'm doing this while I fuck your little girlfriend."

He turns to me. That fear hits me again before becoming hazy, and fatigue runs through me. Despite that, hatred also pushes in. This is why he took me? To make a point to his ex?

I squeeze my eyes closed as warm hands close over my breasts. He then smacks my right breast hard. The pain is muted, but it's also the only thing my body feels besides fuzzy peace.

"No, kitten. You don't get to be asleep for this part. I'm going to fuck you, and when I'm done, you'll be ruined. I'm going to tear into you until you fall apart for me. And once I hold your pieces, I'm never giving them back."

The words send shivers down my spine. Jayden starts to undo his belt.

Rage hovers on the edge of my fog. If I could speak, I'd tell him I meant every word in that video. Tell him I hate him. I feel fuzzy. I hate him? Yes. Hate him.

I ignore the little part of me that is thrilled at his words. That wanted to make him fight to tear me apart. That wanted to... belong. But there is no belonging. He'll use me, and when he's done with me, he'll dump me. Something whispers that he'll maybe even kill me. That seems absurd. I shake my head to think clearly.

Jayden's hot hands land on my shoulders. He slides them down slowly. It makes the hair rise on my skin. He caresses me all over my body. They rub over my ties, pushing me back, making my world rock softly. They rub away the rage and fear and leave me with nothing but fuzzy pleasure. Torturously slowly, they move down. Down to where I'm barred. I try to squeeze my legs together to get some friction, but it doesn't work. His touch feels like static, pinpointed and all over at the same time.

Hot fingers graze my clit, and I jump. Suddenly, he's at my neck, breathing me in, warm breath on my ear. His fingers graze my clit again. Warmth pools in my center. It takes me a minute to realize he's cupping my pussy.

I shake my head. The fog doesn't clear.

He rubs circles around my clit. Forcing sensations into my body. I bite down into the gag. I remember I promised myself I would never come for him again. I think about my old life. About Kyle. About my social media following. About the new series I was going to do, trying food from different cultures.

Jayden is relentless. The sensations are not overbearing, but they're constant. Whatever is going on with me brings my focus right back down to my clit and the pleasure that's being forced on me. There's a wet sucking sound.

"Kitten...you're so wet."

I realize his fingers are in me, gently pushing in and out. He grazes a spot inside me that makes me want to arch my back. He's being gentle and attentive.

Fuck him. I force my mind to think about anything else. Anything.

Warmth brushes my cheek. He's kissing me. I groan, and he pushes his hard, strong body to mine. He's deliciously warm, and I crave that warmth. I didn't realize I was cold until he pressed into me.

He continues playing with me, and heat settles in my core. I feel my muscles clenching and unclenching on his fingers.

"Not yet," he whispers in my ear. "The next time this pretty pussy comes, it's going to be on my cock."

I shake my head. He gently grabs my chin and tilts my face to his. His eyes are warm, and he smiles. It takes my breath away. I've never seen him look so beautiful.

There's pressure on my cunt, and then I feel full. Very, very full. I shift against the sensation. He continues looking into my eyes and brushes a hair away from my face. "You're doing so good."

So good? I shift again. The pressure is still there. Then he starts moving. Slowly thrusting his hips.

Oh shit. He's in me. I rear my head back, but he cups the back of my neck and puts his forehead to mine. I can't move the rest of my body. Gentle thrusts continue, and slowly, my body relaxes, and pleasure fills me.

I blink, and some of the film clears. We're in the entryway to the living room. I move my head and look over his shoulder.

Cole stands behind Sage, hand in her hair, anger in his eyes. He's forcing her to look at us. She has her eyes closed.

I try to cry out. I try to get away. Jayden doesn't let me. He runs his hands down my back and grips my ass. He pulls my ass into him, thrusting a little harder. I whimper.

"Focus on my voice, kitten. Just my voice. You're doing just fine. Your pussy is so wet, so inviting. It's trying to milk my cock. Fuck, I've never felt anything so good." He kisses up along my neck.

No. He's playing a game.

The fluttery kisses continue until he bites down hard. Pain pierces my skin. I cry out through my gag. He's licking the pain away, soothing it with his tongue. "Good girl." He does it again, this time sucking.

I cry out again. My body bucks into him. His thrusts become harder. He reaches a hand down and starts rubbing my clit. That and the pressure makes fire run through my pussy. I clench on him.

"Do you want to come for me, kitten? Want this dick to drive you crazy? It's your dick, kitten. It's yours forever. It'll never belong to anyone else."

I groan. I try to focus on the sound of his voice instead of the sensations, but I'm losing the battle. He's skilled with his fingers and his steady and firm thrusts. He drives me higher and higher.

Finally, I break. I shatter around him, light flashing before my eyes. I've never felt such potent pleasure. It goes on and on. I pulse around him, and he continues to rub and thrust, dragging me out. Finally, I let my head slump against his shoulder.

"Good girl, Jo. You did so well." His voice is tense, and he shudders in me. He picks up his pace. He pounds into me, and I realize just how gentle he was being with me before. His pounding now is brutal, relentless, and claiming. He's huge, and it feels like he's splitting me apart. He groans in my ear, sounding breathless. "Fuck kitten, you're going to make me come."

He slams a few more times, then pushes all the way into me and groans deeply. I feel him pulsing, and heat fills me.

We're both breathing deeply. He pulls my forehead back to his and looks at me.

"Fuck." There's a slight pain in his eyes.

I close my eyes, and my body relaxes. Fatigue fills me, and the haze returns to my mind until I see nothing but static I fall asleep.

~

I'm warm. Deliciously warm. I nestle deeper into that warmth and let out a sigh.

Something shifts behind me. I crack open my eyes. It takes me a second to recognize where I am. Jayden's bed. In the loft. Why am I here?

I roll over. Cole's right there. He smiles. "Hey, little one."

He's the warmth. I frown. "What am I doing here?"

"Cuddling. Which I must say is very uncharacteristic for my snarky girl, but I love it." He pulls me into his body and kisses my forehead.

I push back against him. It is uncharacteristic. How did I get here? I try to remember what happened before.

He sees me furrowing my brows. "Uh oh. Snuggling is about to be over, isn't it?" He grasps my hands and pins them together. "Please don't scratch me, I'm weird about my skincare routine, and you'd put me back at least a week."

I stare at him. He winks.

Flashes of memory roll over me. It comes in bits and pieces, full of fog. I stiffen. Jayden and I did something. Cole was there. Sage was too. Sage. New Year's Eve. My video message to her ex...was Jayden. Him all over me. Touching me. Making me feel good. Making me come.

Cole's grip on my hands tightens just slightly. I cut my gaze around the room and back to him.

"Where is Jayden?" My voice is cold, even to me.

"Out."

"He's too pussy to face me after last night?"

"No. We were running out of groceries since you insisted on feeding that woman."

I glare, but I see the truth in his eyes.

"Let me go."

He hesitates but does.

I sit up. I'm wearing a big black T-shirt. It smells like Jayden. I stand and walk to the balcony, needing space. I see it's snowing outside. The ground is already covered.

"What exactly did he do to me last night?"

Cole is quiet. I turn to look, and he's watching me from the bed. It looks like he's evaluating whether I'll jump from the railing. I think about it. It would ruin whatever plans they have for me, but it's not high enough to do any real damage.

"Why don't you ask him?"

"I'd *like* to, but like you said, he isn't here right now, so I'm asking you."

Cole slowly gets up and approaches me like a wild animal. So he is afraid I'm going to jump.

"He didn't hurt you."

I grit my teeth. "I asked what he did, not what he didn't do."

"Little one..."

"Do I need birth control?"

"What?"

"Do. I. Need. Birth. Control."

He crosses his arms. That's all the answer I need. I feel sick to my stomach. At the same time, I remember the blinding pleasure from last night. How I've never felt like that, not with Kyle, not with any of my exes, and not even giving it to myself. And that scares me.

"I'm going to shower." I don't wait for his reply. I stand in the shower for a long time. The sick feeling doesn't go away. I'm in dangerous territory. I hate these men. Clearly, they are just using me for whatever fucked up plan of revenge they have. But they make me feel better than I ever have, more alive than I ever have. It's intoxicating. It will be so easy for them to lull me into complacency. And they will. They're trying right now.

Why am I still here? Why haven't I tried harder to leave? Something is clearly very wrong with me. Is this Stockholm? It has to be. The thought makes me feel better.

I clean up and get out. I see the tattoo on my back. Their names. It's healing nicely. It makes me mad. It's okay. I'll get it removed as soon as I get away. I know a good place. Kyle had to get a hand tattoo removed for his job. It's not a big deal.

I wrap a towel around myself and run up the cold steps to my room. I get dressed and come back out.

Jayden is back, and he and Cole are bringing in and unloading groceries. The breeze through the door is brutal, and my wet hair makes it worse.

"I got you more of your meals." Jayden shuts the door and drops off the last of the bags on the island. They're Walmart bags. I wonder how far away the store is. How long has he been gone?

"Thanks."

I see him throw me a glance while wiping the snow off his hair. I ignore him and start helping put the groceries away.

"You're going to need to let her in," I state.

He grunts.

"It's too cold outside. She'll die before you can fuck with her anymore. I'm assuming that's why I'm still alive. You aren't done with either of us."

Jayden calmly pulls out a bag of apples. "No. You're alive because you belong to us."

"Yeah, yeah, I'm yours, whatever." I stop and catch his glance. "Oh, I forgot. I have HIV. Serves you right." I don't, but I want him to live in a little fear.

He laughs a deep, gravelly sound. Cole chuckles too.

"And I expect you to go back and get me Plan B."

Silence. Jayden has stilled. I look at him, and his demeanor has totally changed. He looks deadly. He doesn't move toward me, but I feel I need to take a step back.

"No."

"No?" Outrage flushes my cheeks. "You don't get to decide, no," I sputter. "It's my body. I won't want to be pregnant, especially with," I wave my hands at him, "you."

He snatches me up around the neck. His hand is firm but not painful. His voice is measured and angry, and it makes me shiver. "You'll do whatever I decide, kitten. If I want to see you carrying my child, then I will. If I want to get you birth control, then I will. You belong to me. And I said no. Don't question me again." He lets me go.

Fear and anger mix in a heady cocktail. That and...lust. Jesus, what the fuck is wrong with me? I tamp those feelings down.

Jayden continues with the food. "Cole, bring Sage in. We'll move the kitten to my room. She makes a good point. Don't want her freezing to death just yet."

Cole nods and whistles as he goes outside.

In the evening, Jayden makes me stay in bed with him since Sage is in my room. Cole also joins us, so I'm sandwiched between the two of them. Jayden said he can't trust I won't run again. He's not wrong. I lay awake the first night, tense, ready for them to make a move. But they don't. And they don't the next night or the next. They keep a close eye on me, always having one or the other within hearing distance. Anytime I try to snoop around, they follow me.

I keep trying to talk to Sage, but they keep her doped up. Maybe so she won't talk to me, I'm not sure. She stares at the wall with a glazed expression. She doesn't even want to eat. I worry. She doesn't have much weight to drop. I try to force water down her, and she sometimes accepts that. They've also taken my paper clip and all the rest in Cole's room.

Cole lets me whittle when he's around. I use the knife that he seems to have an emotional connection to. I pry him for more information, but he says he'll answer if we fuck. So I leave it alone.

This becomes increasingly difficult as every time I'm around either of them with their strong bodies and handsome faces, my cunt practically purrs. I try to get her on board with the kidnapping and lack of morals, but she doesn't get the message.

I mostly sit in Sage's room, staring at the wall, wondering what I can do. I fight the realization that their defenses are down the most when mine are. Which means I have to let my guard down to get anywhere. Or at least pretend to. Carefully, because they seem to be able to sniff out a lie from a mile away.

I fight the idea of getting in bed with the devil. I'm worried I won't make it out if I do. But I also worry I won't make it out if I don't. Clearly, I haven't gotten anywhere by fighting them. Well, I have gotten somewhere. Fucked. Maybe it's time to try something else. It's not just me I'm fighting for anymore. It's Sage too.

On the evening of the fourth night, since Sage came inside, I convinced them to let me help her shower. She's started to smell, and I can tell it annoys Jayden. He helps carry her downstairs and sits her down on the shower floor.

"Make sure she doesn't drown. She doesn't get to get off that easy." He stalks off.

Sage raises a weak hand and flips him the bird. But he's already gone. I try to get her out of the shower so I can warm up the water, but she's dead weight.

"Sorry, girl, it's going to be cold at first." She doesn't even flinch when the water hits her. Soon, it warms and fills the room with steam. I consider Jayden's words. If he has worse plans for her than drowning, maybe it would be a mercy to let her go.

I widen my eyes, realizing where my mind went. Did I just consider murdering someone? I feel like throwing up.

"He's a dick," Sage slurs out.

I startle and look down at her. "Yeah."

She has her eyes closed, lashes dark against her cheek, and her head leaned back against the wall. I shampoo her hair as best I can, getting soaked in the process.

I can't take the silence anymore. I ask, "What did he do to you?"

The water patters down on her face. For a while, I think she's going to ignore me like every other time. Until she speaks. "He told me he didn't want me," she grimaces. "He couldn't stand to look at me. That I'm a whore and a slut, and the world would be better off without me." She cracks her eyes open and looks at me. Really looks at me for the first time. Her eyes are slightly glazed. "Don't let him hurt you. He'll get close to you and then break your heart." She closes her eyes. "It's a game to him. You need to get as far away from him as you can."

I swallow. "How long were you together?"

"Nine years."

A pang shoots through me. It almost feels like jealousy. I stamp it down.

"Nine years." She goes on, her voice wistful. "I met him before he went to the police academy. He convinced me to quit my job and live with him. Said he'd provide for me." She laughs softly. "I was an idiot."

I stare at the steam that billows off her body and the floor.

"When he dumped me, I had nothing."

The water falls like rain for a while. It starts to cool.

"Why are they giving you drugs?"

She laughs. "I got clean a year ago. Broke my back when I was a teen and got prescribed Percocet. Got addicted. Cleaned my life up before he broke up with me. Apparently, that makes him mad."

Rage fills me.

She looks at me with tired eyes. "Girl, you're hot. You could have anyone. Why him?"

I grit my teeth. "I didn't have a choice."

"Ah yes, love will make you do crazy things." She closes her eyes.

"It's not love!"

She doesn't answer. She's clearly not going to believe me. And I don't know that I entirely blame her. Jayden seems to be doing his best to convince her we are together.

Which we aren't.

We sit in silence for a while. The water gets icy, and I turn it off. I get Cole to help me carry her back upstairs.

Sage is not doing well. What else does he have planned for her? The dread that has been lurking the past few days fills me. What else does he have planned for me?

## 23

Our kitten sleeps between us again, where she belongs. She refused to touch us the first night, but she's gotten more relaxed now, not going stiff every time our skin brushes. It feels nice in a way I didn't expect. I find myself relaxing around her.

I pull her soft, sexy body into me. I can't get enough of her soft curves, her silky skin, and the little hairs on the back of her neck. She makes a mewling sound that turns me on and starts to wriggle away.

"No." I clamp her down. I need her tonight. My heart has been racing all day. I've been trying not to think about it, but my mind keeps hijacking my control.

I fall asleep with her tucked into me.

I wake up, and she's gone. I'm in my mom's living room, with its maroon and green decor and live-laugh-love signs.

Panic runs through me, and I start to sweat. Something is wrong. Something is very wrong. I look around the small room. No one is here with me. I need to get there in time. I need to hurry. I run down to her room and find her before I get there.

She's lying on the ground, half out of the bathroom. She's face up, her eyes are open, and her lips are blue.

"No!" I drop to my knees beside her and start CPR. She's cold. I feel her ribs crack beneath my hands. No, no, no, I wasn't in time. There's a pill bottle on the sink. It's Advil, but I know what she actually keeps in there.

"Fuck. Come back to me, Mom."

As I work on her, suddenly, a wound opens up in her chest. A gunshot wound. Her blood is hot on my hands.

I jerk back. I stand, only to realize I'm in uniform. The person lying in front of me isn't my mother; it's the man I shot. My gun is in my hand. I smell gunpowder.

More people show up, coming from the rooms down the hall.

"He shot him."

"Killed him!"

My chest heaves for breath. This isn't how it happened.

Suddenly, I'm in a courtroom. The same courtroom I sent criminals to. Only I'm behind the desk before the judge. And the judge is the man I killed. The man who pulled a gun on me and tried to shoot me that one night at work.

He stands and points at me. "Guilty! This man is a murderer. Guilty!"

I panic. I know he's about to pull a gun. I know I have to kill him before he kills me. But where's my gun? I scramble to find it. *Where is my gun?*

# Mary Jo

## 24

I'm startled awake by Jayden jumping out of bed. He flies to the closet, flinging the doors open. He's breathing hard like he just ran a marathon.

Cole shoots up beside me.

"Gun, where's the gun," Jayden mutters. He's shirtless, and his back glints with sweat.

"Fuck." Cole jumps up and darts over to Jayden. "Leave it alone, man. It's not real."

Jayden swings for Cole, who ducks and puts his hands up. "It's me. You're having a flashback. You're safe."

Jayden's gaze bounces around wildly. He looks right through us. He then goes back to the closet.

"Jayden!" Cole grabs his arm, and Jayden flings him off almost faster than I can track and throws him on the bed. He starts rummaging faster. I hear beeping.

"Shit." Cole jumps up and pulls me to the other side of the room, putting himself between Jayden and me.

Jayden swings around, a pistol in his hand.

I freeze. The pistol is black and matte, with iron sights. He briefly flags us with it before pointing it around the room. He had a gun in this place the whole time?

"Where is he?" Jayden's chest heaves.

Cole freezes. I've never seen the look in Jayden's eyes before. He looks like a cornered animal. He looks...afraid.

"Don't move," Cole whispers to me. "He won't hurt you."

I'm not so sure. And the look on Cole's face tells me he's not so sure either.

"Where is he?" Jayden demands again.

"He's not here. He's dead. You're having a flashback."

Jayden looks at us, and for a second, I think he really sees us. He takes a step back. Then he starts wildly looking around again.

"Jayden," Cole whispers.

Jayden jumps and looks back at us. "What are you doing here?"

"You're at the cabin. They aren't here. They're dead. You had a bad dream."

Jayden trembles. He runs a hand through his hair and blinks. He lowers the gun to his side.

"Give it to me," Cole demands.

Jayden stiffens. Cole walks slowly up to him, still keeping his body between us. "You're safe. I'll keep you safe."

He shudders and hands the gun over. Cole puts it in the closet again and sits next to Jayden on the bed.

I'm still standing there. The two talk in low tones. I tiptoe downstairs and curl up on the couch. I wasn't supposed to see that. I wasn't supposed to see any of that.

# COLE

**25**

THE FREEZING WIND WHIPS AROUND MY FACE. I TAKE THE first draw on my cigarette. Jayden went for a run with no coat on in the dead of night. My fingers shake, needing that hit. It's been a long time since I've craved a cigarette this badly.

Jo is asleep on the couch, but I stay on the front doorstep just in case she decides to try and leave. The weather instantly makes my fingers burn. I embrace it.

It's been a long time since I've seen Jayden like this. He was always stoic. I'm hit with a memory of us as seven-year-olds, playing by the river. He brought his Gameboy with the red case, which I was insanely jealous of, and I watched him play for hours. Even when he'd win, he'd always keep a calm demeanor while I'd hoot and holler.

I take another draw, and the cherry lights up, warm and alive. I didn't know at the time that the Gameboy was a sick sort of gift from Pat. Not until I got my own. Not until he told me to start making him feel good.

I let out a heavy breath. I'm not even the one who had a nightmare, and I feel jittery. Jayden is usually the one looking after me, not the other way around.

I grimace, thinking about right before Christmas. I almost lost him. It's been about the three-month anniversary of his mom's death, and revenge was the only thing that saved his life.

I reach the end of my cigarette. I stand in the blistering cold for a long time, lost in memories. So long that I startle when Jayden jogs up.

"What are you doing?" he snaps.

"Smoking." I realize just how cold it is when it's hard to move my face.

"You're going to get frostbite; get inside." He moves past me to open the door. He has no shirt on, and his skin is pink and steaming.

"You too," I grumble.

The heat is almost oppressive when we get inside. Jayden looks over at the couch and quietly moves around the kitchen, grabbing a protein bar. He glances at me and then clasps the back of my neck. "You good?" He searches my eyes. He's always been able to read me by just looking at me.

I look away. "Yeah, I'm fine. Are you okay?"

He doesn't let go. I keep avoiding his gaze until he gives me a warm squeeze.

I look up. There's affection and concern in his eyes. "You okay?" he asks again.

"Yeah, man." I give a small smile.

He keeps searching, and then his gaze shutters. He turns away and throws the protein bar onto the counter. "I thought I was over it. I've been doing a lot better. It won't happen again."

"Hey," I say loudly, then look over to make sure I didn't wake Jo. I say quieter, "I'm good. Don't worry about me."

He also looks over at the couch. There's a haunted look in his eyes. "There's something I have to do today. Keep her distracted."

I just nod. I see when his walls settle fully down again and when anger takes over. "I'm gonna shower."

I shrug out of my coat and go to the couch. I sit on the unoc-cupied one and watch Jo's chest rise and fall. She has a tank on, and I can see her breasts gently swelling underneath. Her pink lips are slightly pouty, and her lashes are dark against her skin. She looks so peaceful. So innocent. How did she get tangled up with fucked-up assholes like us?

# Mary Jo

### 26

---

I STAY DOWNSTAIRS ALL NIGHT. I HEAR THE FRONT DOOR
open and close, and then it's still for a long time. At some point, I
fall asleep, and when I wake up, the cabin is still. Too still. I feel
like I'm being watched.

I sit bolt upright. I'm on the couch, and it's daylight out. My
gaze darts around the room until it lands on Cole, standing
deadly still, grinning at me. He's by the fireplace, wearing a dark
blue t-shirt and jeans that stretch across his thick thighs.

The hair on the back of my neck stands up.

"She awakens."

"What are you doing? Where's Jayden?" I try to move slowly.
I feel like I'm being stalked by a predator, and any move will set
him off. I scan my surroundings. The knife I've been using to
whittle is on the coffee table by me.

He sees me notice it, and his eyes light up. He looks feral.
"Let's play a game."

"No." My voice is quiet. My heart pounds. "Where's
Jayden?" I ask again.

He laughs. "He won't protect you. Plus, he's out with Sage."

What? My hands shake.

"Oh, don't worry, he's not going to fuck her. He saves that for you."

I tell myself I don't care about that.

Cole continues smiling at me, his face handsome and mean. "The game is keep away. You keep that pretty body away from me, and you win."

"What? I—"

"You get the knife." He nods at the table.

He'd let me kill him? I look at the knife. I've used it before. Or at least, I tried to.

"If I get three cuts, I'm done. You win."

Adrenaline fills my body. "If I win, you let me go."

He throws his head back and laughs. "You drive a hard bargain. Okay, I accept."

Fuck. I don't like how easily he agreed. I clarify, "You let me go home. Right after."

"Okay." He's still smiling.

"Swear it. On your mom."

His grin freezes for a second. Then he does a slow, flourishing bow. "I swear on my mom that if you win, I'll let you go. Right after."

Excitement courses through me. The thrill of the fight. The possibility of escape. I snatch up the knife.

His voice goes low. "Better run, little one."

I do. I take off to the basement, to Cole's room. I hear his measured footsteps behind me. He's not even rushing. I slam his door shut and lock it. The light is off, and I keep it that way. I scramble for the desk. It's heavy as fuck. My heart is pounding, and I shove it. It moves a little. I put my whole body into it and shove it against the door.

The door handle rattles. He's fiddling with the lock. I struggle to inch the desk close enough that the door has no give. The door opens an inch before slamming into the desk.

There's a dark chuckle. "What a smart girl. Useless, but cute."

I look around and heave in a breath. All I need to do is cut him three times. If I can lure him close enough to the crack, I can do that.

The hallway light flips off. I'm plunged into darkness. I blink, trying to keep my heart rate even. There's silence. Slowly, a little light from upstairs filters into the room.

Something crashes into the door so loud my ears ring. I jump, stepping back.

*Crash.* It happens again. It sounds like he's throwing his whole body into the wood.

"Lemon Drrrrop."

*Crash.* Wood splinters, and the desk moves a few inches.

His voice remains even. "Let me innnn. I'm going to do violent things to that pretty body."

I shiver and adjust my grip on the knife. My hand is sweaty. It's darker in here than it is out there. I position myself behind the door so I can stab him when he comes in. Maybe I can get an organ or an artery.

*Crash.* The desk scoots again. There's enough room to slip through.

He's silent this time. I ready myself to slash whatever part of him I see first.

There's a hiss, and suddenly, the doorway goes cloudy. I can't see anything in the cloud and darkness. I take a step back, trying to figure out what the cloud is.

"Hello." The voice is right by me. I scream and slash out with the knife, making contact. There's a grunt.

I slash back and forth again, but there's no resistance this time. Another hiss and a blowing sound, and the air in front of me is murky again. I cough and back up.

Something clatters to the ground, and my back is slammed into the wall. My head bounces off it painfully. I slash out again and make contact with something. I cough against the film in the air.

He groans, but it sounds...turned on. I tear my hand back again, but it's also slammed into the wall. I feel like my front is up against a solid wall of muscle.

"Mmmm. Little one."

"Fuck you. *Fuck you.*" I struggle to free my hand. Desperation fills me. This is my chance. I have to win this. I have to get away.

His body moves on me. He shrugs out of something, a jacket sleeve, then pins my knife hand with his knee. I jerk it away, but he presses harder, making me cry out in pain.

"Easy, little one. Be still." I still and feel the pain radiating from my wrist, his bone digging into me. He shrugs the rest of the jacket off and replaces his knee with his hand. A jacket. He wasn't wearing a jacket before. He must have put it on to get an advantage.

"You cheated!" I try to head-butt him, but I can't get much leverage. His body heat sinks into me, traveling lower.

"How?" He ducks his head to my neck and pulls in a deep breath. His beard tickles my skin.

"The jacket!"

"First," he grinds his hips into me, "there were no rules against that. And second," he grinds again, "you got me through it. Bloodthirsty girl." His voice rattles through his chest and into me. I smell spearmint.

"Fuck. You. I'm done playing your stupid game. Let me go home."

"Pfft. Although you did make the chase fun. You deserve a reward for that."

He strips the knife from my hand faster than I can stop him. He flicks it up to my neck, and I freeze. The metal is cold against my skin. I feel my heartbeat pounding against it.

Cole leans to the other side of my neck. I feel his hot tongue lick from the base up to my ear. Goosebumps prickle on my body.

"Yes. Let's make this pretty thing feel good. Too much stress lately." He steps back until the only thing touching me is the knife. "Get on the bed."

As soon as he lets up, I duck under him and try for the door. He snatches me by the hair and flings me back. I bounce on the bed. He's on top of me in a flash. The knife is back at my throat, and I feel a small, white-hot line of pain there. Fuck, the knife is digging into my throat.

"My god," he groans. "Were you made just for me? You're perfect. I love it when you fight."

I look into his eyes. They're alive with light and lust. He looks devastating. Against all reason, my core feels wet.

He pulls the knife back, ducks down, and licks across the cut he made. It stings, and he sucks, his groan vibrating my neck. Pleasure zips down my spine.

Cole rips my leggings off. I try to scoot away. He rips my shirt off, tearing it in half. He yanks my bra away from my skin and cuts it off as well. Soon, I lay naked in front of him, his body between me and the door. He adjusts his cock in his pants. I see a wet mark on his torso on the right side. No, not wet. Blood.

He sees where I'm looking. "Jayden's little kitten has claws." He licks his lips, and his gaze bores into me. "You can mark me anytime you like."

My mouth drops open. He drops to his knees between my legs, knife hand going between my thighs. I stiffen.

He groans, "You're so wet for me already. Do you like to feel afraid, little one?"

I close my eyes. I feel something hard against my clit, and I jump.

"Oh no, don't move right now. I would hate to cut this pretty body without meaning to."

I freeze. He has the knife to my cunt. The thought is both

terrifying and heady. The cold metal rubs down my clit. I look and see he has the blunt edge against me. I can't look away. He draws it down over me again and uses his other finger to push into my pussy. It fills me with sensation, and I groan. He pulls out and spreads the juices on the blade. It glints in the low light.

"You're...sick." I tremble.

"You like sick." His smile doesn't reach his eyes. He looks devastating. He brings the knife to my lips. "Taste yourself."

When I don't open, he shoves the blunt end of the blade between my lips. His voice is low with warning. "Taste. Yourself."

I stick my tongue out and touch the tip to the blunt side. Metal, blood, and my own taste coat my lips and fill my mouth.

Cole groans. With one hand, he pulls his pants down and lines himself up with my entrance. Even in the low light, he looks so big. I try to back up, but he presses the blade to my mouth in warning. He pushes the head in slowly, and I feel myself stretch around him. I moan.

"What a good girl." He holds himself there. He shakes, holding still. Slowly, he pushes in. I'm wet, but the stretch is uncomfortable. I shift to try and accommodate him but stop when I feel the metal move against my mouth. He grins and pushes in more and more until he's seated in me. He drops his head to my forehead. "Christ."

My chest heaves beneath him. I feel so full around him. He waits there, also breathing heavily. I feel my hot breath fog up the knife against my lips.

Slowly, he starts moving, thrusting shallowly. Soon, I don't feel the stretch, and I feel myself getting wetter.

"You feel so goddamn good. Your cunt is like heaven." He moves the knife to my neck and lightly places it there.

His dick rubs gently on the spot inside me, which makes me want to arch my back. He keeps at it, driving me crazy. He reaches his other hand down and tweaks my nipple.

I groan. He starts thrusting harder. "Fuck." He rolls my nipple between his fingers and then bends down to suck it. I arch into him, the feeling potent.

"Such gorgeous tits."

My pussy makes wet sounds. He easily moves in and out of me now, every thrust lightly tapping the knife on my skin, reminding me it's there. Pleasure and fear fill me. A man with a knife who clearly gets off on pain is fucking me.

And I love it.

I reach up and rake my fingers down his shirt and chest. He stiffens. I do it hard enough to draw blood and make eye contact with him. I say between thrusts, "For your... skincare...routine."

He laughs and grabs my neck with a huge hand, not cutting off my air but threatening to. He brings the knife to his mouth and licks up the blade. That makes him pound harder, his face fierce.

"Play with yourself, little one. That's your reward for being such a good girl."

I slip my hand down my stomach, knowing I can't fight him on this. That he'll make me come regardless, so I may as well get as much pleasure out of it as I can. It doesn't take long, and I feel an orgasm building. Cole tightens his hand as I tighten around his cock, and it heightens the sensations. Soon, I come around him. The hand around my throat garbles my cry.

"Filthy slut. Coming on my dick like a good girl."

His words only make me come harder. He continues to pound into me. Once I come down, I take the hand that was on my pussy and put it to my lips. I lick my fingers off, giving him a mocking look.

Cole groans and pounds harder into me. I take that hand and feel down his chest until I find the wet mark where I cut him. I dig my fingers in.

He roars, slamming into me so hard my head bounces back

against the wall. I feel a second orgasm come on quickly. Cole grips my chin and spits into my mouth.

My orgasm slams into me. It's harder than the last one, coming in waves of electrifying pleasure. He also comes, pressing his body into mine and pulsing.

I gasp. When I come down off my high, I realize he's still in me. I shove at him. He only growls and pushes in harder, claiming me and pinning me under him.

I realize there is warm wetness around my neck. What is that? Holy shit, is that blood? I reach my hand up.

Cole pulls out and gets up off me, turning the light on. I blink and look at my hand. There's blood all over it. Oh my god. I'm bleeding pretty badly.

"Easy lemon drop, that's not from you."

I look up to see Cole has blood dripping down his forearm from a slash on his upper arm. He grins at me. "That was hot."

"Holy shit, you're bleeding."

He looks at his arm briefly. "Happens when you play with knives." He walks up to me and tilts my head up with a finger, looking at my neck. "Let's get this washed out."

As he brings me to the bathroom, I see white powder on the floor and a fire extinguisher. That bastard.

I go to the sink in the bathroom, but he turns the shower on. "Shower."

I want to argue, but I still have endorphins flowing through me, and a shower sounds amazing. I see him stripping his clothes off. "No."

He shakes his head. "I won't do anything, little one. Get in."

I glare at him. But I can't stop him or what he has planned. I get in the hot water, and it feels like heaven.

I let out a small groan.

"Hush." He steps in after me and looks at me with lust. I see he's getting hard again.

I turn away and stick my face in the water, letting it run

through my hair. There's the snap of a bottle opening, and then I feel Cole's hands on my back. I stiffen.

"Just washing," he murmurs.

"I can do that."

"I know you can." He keeps rubbing the soap on my body. It's spearmint-scented and smells like him. He scrubs methodically, getting my arms, paying close attention to the cut on my neck, careful not to get soap in it. He washes my tits and between my legs but those movements are methodical and not sensual. As he bends down to get my legs, I see hash marks of scars all over his back.

I draw in a sharp breath.

He jerks his gaze up to my face. "Did I hurt you?"

"No." I stare at him. Understanding flashes across his face, but he doesn't say anything. He turns me away from him and massages soap into my hair.

What the hell. Where did he get those? They're long but old, raised and white. They almost look like...he was whipped.

His hands are big and gentle. "I can hear your brain running. Stop that. It's not a story you want to hear." He continues massaging. It feels good, and my scalp is tingling. At this moment, I don't want him to stop.

But he has to. I start to come to my senses, and for the first time, I don't want to. I'd like to just pretend this was hot sex with a hot guy. Pretend like he isn't riddled with signs of abuse. Pretend I'm in the comfort of my own home. Like there isn't a girl being force-fed drugs upstairs. Like one of the guys who kidnapped her, one of the guys who kidnapped me didn't think about shooting me last night. That they aren't both batshit crazy.

I get out of the shower and see that Cole is still rock hard. And it makes heat flow through me again. I desperately need to distract myself from that and...everything.

"You'll need to bandage that arm." I eye him. He has red

scratches down his chest and an oozing cut on his abdomen. "And that."

He doesn't even look at them. "I've had worse."

"That's not what I said," I mutter. As I wrap a towel around myself, I see he's smirking at me.

Oh god. It sounded like I cared there for a second. I glare at him, "But if you want to get an infection, by all means. Go ahead. It'll make my life easier. I don't even know why I suggested it in the first place."

I march back to his room, where I find my shirt has been destroyed. I yank my pants on. "I only had three, and now I have two. Cocksucker."

He follows me, chuckling, "I'll buy you more 'cause I don't plan on stopping."

I march past him and upstairs to the loft to get another shirt. By the time I come back downstairs, Cole is dressed in only his pants, his muscled chest on display.

I'm starving. I go through the fridge to see what we have. I end up pouring myself a bowl of cereal and groan when I take the first bite. It has that perfect crunch, and none of it has gone soggy. The food is heaven.

Cole also pours himself a bowl, and we eat in silence. I finish my first and go for another.

"Who was Jayden looking for last night?" I pour my milk, and Cole snatches it from me before I can finish it. I glare at him. He uses the rest in his bowl.

"Not sure which one."

"Which one?" I look at him.

He looks at me for a second, then tosses the empty milk container at the trash. It misses and clatters to the ground.

"Someone scared him. Hurt him."

"Yes." He looks into my eyes.

"What happened?"

He cocks an eyebrow. "Why don't you ask him?"

I scoff, but Cole looks serious.

"Ask the man who kidnapped his ex, forced her to relapse, and snatched me up just to play games with her head?"

"There's more than that."

"Then tell me!"

He takes another bite and chews slowly. "Sage is not innocent, little one. Everything that goes around comes around."

"Am I innocent?" The blood pounds in my ears.

He gives me a long look, staring into my soul. "Yes."

"Then why am I here?"

"Because you got caught up in some shit that you shouldn't have. And when you did, you caught his eye. And then you caught mine."

I search his blue eyes. He doesn't look away. My heart is racing. "Will you ever let me go?" All the other times, I knew what the answer to that question would be. This time, it feels like he'll be honest with me. Which makes me want to throw up.

Cole doesn't respond. Just stares. There's heat and gentleness and...possession in his eyes.

Anger rolls through me. "Will you ever let me go, Cole? You said I'm innocent. You know I don't belong here. You can make it right. Let me go home."

He stands and walks slowly over to me. He tilts my chin up with his finger and drifts his lips down. They brush mine. "No, little one. No, I don't think I will."

## 27

I push Sage to her knees in the dirt. She hasn't stopped crying since I dragged her out into the woods. Probably thinks I'm going to kill her. I've thought about it. But not here.

"This is it," I say, my voice monotone.

She sobs, her clothes dirty and hair tangled, kneeling with her face close to the dirt. She's so pitiful it makes me angry. If she was my kitten, she'd fight me, cuss me out, make me bleed. But Sage has never been strong.

I yank my hand in her hair and make her look at the boulder under the oak tree. "Here we are. The sad, sad end to a sad, sad man."

She blinks tears out of her eyes, barely registering. I cut her off cold Turkey from her pills, so she's withdrawing pretty hard. Her whole body shakes.

"He died in the end like he lived—like a coward. Don't worry. We cut off his dick and balls before he went. Stuck them in his eye sockets. While he was still alive, naturally."

She leans over and pukes. I cross my arms. "Sorry to defile the things you liked. But he liked to stick them in little boys too, so he just couldn't keep them."

She hasn't looked up from her vomiting. Her breathing is fast and shallow. I curl my lip in disgust and yank her up by her hair. I put my mouth to her ear and say, "This is where I put the people who cross me." She struggles weakly. "Say hello to your final resting place. Not today, but soon. Should I bury you with his fingers in your pussy? What's left of them anyway. Would you like to wear his wedding ring too? Since you seemed to want to play his girl."

She smells of vomit. I set her back down.

Her lack of response fills me with disappointment. It feels disrespectful. What, with her being in such an important place. The last time I was here, Cole and I achieved true justice. Not the justice they preach from behind the badge. But the real kind.

Right now, I feel nothing of the relief and triumph I felt before. The quivering girl at my feet just annoys me. I came out here to achieve some sort of equilibrium, and Sage isn't giving it.

I fling Sage over my shoulder, more than a little mad that she is making my revenge feel empty. I don't want to keep feeling. I've done enough over the past 24 hours. Things were not going to plan. Actually, the only really interesting thing after taking Sage has been watching my kitten try to fight for both of them. Watching her hatred deepen. Watching that pretty little mouth pucker when I come around. It does things to my dick and my mind. I can't stop thinking about her. Her fiery spirit, her hate-filled eyes, and her sexy body.

My dick gets hard, and I feel a spark of passion. What would she look like taking Cole and me at the same time? Stretched around both of us with that perfect, tight little body. Would she kick and claw? Pretend she hated it when she secretly loved every second?

I grin and walk quickly toward the cottage.

# Mary Jo

## 28

JAYDEN STOMPS INTO THE CABIN, CARRYING SAGE. HE TAKES her to her room and comes back out. I look up from where I was reading a book on the couch. As he's taking off his coat, his gaze zeroes in on my neck. The air shifts, and he's to me before I realize he's moving. He snatches my chin and tilts my head back.

"What. Happened," he growls.

I try to get away, but his fingers on my chin are firm, although gentle.

"It was nothing."

He lets my head tilt back down to look into my eyes. "Answer."

Cole pipes up from the kitchen. "That was me. We played with knives."

"Fuck." Jayden runs a hand through his hair. "Jesus, Cole, you know how dangerous that is."

"Yes, mother." I see Cole roll his eyes from here. "If you don't like that, then you won't even want to hear about what she did to me."

Jayden cuts his glance to me. "I hope she fucked your ass to teach you a lesson." He's looking at me with passion and heat.

My eyebrows shoot up. Cole laughs. A hint of a smirk crosses Jayden's face, and then his eyes darken. He stands up straighter and suddenly seems to loom over me.

I swallow. His eyes dart to the movement, and he smirks fully this time.

"Let's play another game, Cole." Jayden keeps his eyes locked on me. Cole comes up beside him.

The two men look lethal, standing next to each other. Even though Cole and I just fucked, I feel lust roll through me again. Jayden's fingers flex almost imperceptibly.

I stand slowly. Cole's nostrils flare.

"Let's see how much of us she can take at once."

Both of them? At the same time? Fuck no. I look around for something, anything, while trying to keep an eye on both of them. I know if I run, I might as well lay down right here and spread my legs.

Jayden moves slightly to my left, and I take a small step away. They begin to separate, trying to get my back. I inch away, keeping both of them in my sights.

"What's the matter, little one? Sore?" Cole steps in front of my access to the kitchen. If I wanted to get there, I'd need to jump the couch, and he'd be able to get me with his long arms.

"No." I inch toward the stairs. "That would require your dick to be big enough to feel."

Cole laughs, but it's dark. Jayden continues towards me on my left.

My foot hits a step. When it does, a feral smile lights up Jayden's face, and I realize they've been herding me here. Anger flashes through me, and I clench my fists.

"I'll hold her down while you punish that nasty mouth," Jayden growls.

I inch up a step. "How about you just beat your sorry dicks in the shower. It's not my fault you can't get pussy unless it's forced."

Jayden lunges at me, but I'm expecting it, and I dart up the stairs. They're fast, but they have extra muscle holding them down. I go for the railing, intending to jump off it onto the couch, but an arm wraps around my middle, and I'm flying through the air. I land on the bed with a bounce.

Both of them loom over the end of the bed. I glare at them.

"Forced? I'll have you begging for this dick, kitten."

Cole begins stripping his shirt off, baring his muscled chest and angry cuts.

"I'll never beg you," I spit.

Arousal flashes in both their eyes, and I feel my pussy throb. I'm already soaked.

"That tone, kitten." Jayden's voice is full of dry warning. "I'll give you one chance to apologize for being a brat."

I know I'm playing with fire. I know the only logical thing to do is apologize and beg them to go easy on me. Instead, I listen to the thrill running in my blood. The heady horniness fills me, and I say, "Suck my dick."

They move so fast that I can't track them. Suddenly, I'm on my back, and my head is yanked back so all I see is Cole. He's pulling his pants down, and his dick is out. He laughs, "I love that smart mouth."

"Put that dick anywhere near my mouth, and I'll bite it off."

He throws his head back and groans. His dick bobs in my face. My pants are ripped off. I look down and see Jayden fisting my shirt.

"Don—"

He rips it off as well.

"Fuck you." I go to cover my breasts, and he slaps my hands away. I kick at him, feeling the slickness between my thighs. He fights me away like I'm an annoying fly and lines himself up with my entrance. I push backward, but he slams into me.

Pain locks into my core. I cry out. Jayden pulls back and slams in again. I'm wet, and he slides in easier this time. I kick against the pain, trying to get away, but he doesn't let up. It feels like he's hitting my cervix with a hammer.

Jayden locks eyes with me. "That pain is for threatening to bite his dick off, kitten." He pauses inside of me. "What are you going to do?"

I grit my teeth.

He pulls out and slams back in again, white-hot heat jolting through me.

"I'm not apologizing."

Cole taps my cheek. I glare up at him. He's fisting his cock. "If and when I choose to forgive you, I'll paint your pretty little face with my cum. Open up."

Jayden starts gently moving in and out of me. The pain starts to get mixed with pleasure with a sense of fullness. It feels amazing. I stare daggers at Cole. It makes him grin harder. He forces the tip between my lips. I'm so tempted to open and bite down.

Jayden gives a small sound of warning. I open all the way, and Cole shoves in. I let him and am overwhelmed with both of them at once. Cole starts moving across my tongue, his musk filling my mouth. There's a thrill to taking them both at the same time. To have two men chasing their pleasure with me. Two very hot men.

They start at the same pace, slow and gentle. It's dirty and hot and so wrong. That just turns me on more. I reach up and grab Cole by the base and squeeze hard.

He groans and slams into my mouth and down my throat. Jayden follows suit, and I gag while the sensation overwhelms me. They pick up at a faster pace, and slapping fills the air. I can't breathe.

"Little slut just wants to be used for her holes?" Cole grunts. "Just wants us to work her body to get off?"

Pleasure shoots down my center, and I feel myself get wetter. Jayden's fingers dig into my hips, both painful and pleasurable. "God. So wet," his voice rumbles.

Cole pulls out for a quick second, enough for me to breathe, then tilts my head back to get better access to my throat. Jayden continues pounding, bouncing my whole body with his force. Cole gives me a wicked look before pushing back into my mouth. "She's wet because I just came inside her not even an hour ago."

"Oh yeah?" Jayden's fingers dig deeper, and I groan. "Once wasn't enough for her, huh? She needs to be reminded over and over again about who she belongs to."

The words fill me with forbidden pleasure. I feel fingers on my clit at the same time that Cole reaches down and flicks my nipple. I arch my back and moan around Cole's dick. He moans back, stuttering a little in his thrusts.

"I wonder," Jayden says. "Have you ever had anyone back here?" I feel fingers at my ass. They wiggle to my hole and play there.

I struggle against the foreign sensation and try to pull Cole out of my mouth.

"Nuh-uh." He pushes in so deep I gag repeatedly. He lets me get two deep breaths, then goes back to sliding deeply in and out of my throat. The fingers at my ass continue. It feels odd, but it's not bad.

"Who has filled you here before, kitten?"

Cole pulls out, and I heave in breaths. I look down at Jayden. He looks slightly angry.

"No one." I lick my lips.

The look clears slightly. "No one, hmmm?" A finger presses against my entrance, and I stiffen. "Relax, kitten. Tensing makes it worse."

"I don't like anal."

Cole leans down and starts sucking a nipple into his mouth and plays with my clit. Despite my tension, it feels good. Cole keeps at it until I relax slightly.

"How do you know you don't like it unless you've tried it?" Jayden slowly pushes. I cry out and kick back, but he just follows, slowly pumping his dick. The fingers at my clit don't let up. I feel Cole's dick pulsing on my skin.

"Grab me, little one."

I do. I grip him hard and rub my hand up and down his shaft in punishing strokes. I let my nails scratch him a little. I'm angry, but pleasure fills me as they continue to work me. The finger at my exit starts to feel good, adding pressure that I'm not used to feeling, but also pulses of pleasure.

"Good girl. Take the whole thing."

They work me higher and higher. I'm about to come when Jayden pulls out of me completely.

I groan. Cole takes his place and slips into me.

"Clean yourself off me." Jayden takes his place by my head. I do, scraping my teeth slightly, just enough he thinks it's an accident. Just as I start to feel tingles again, they switch again.

I know what they're doing now. Jayden grins at me. They keep going, and I try to mask every time they drive me close, but it's like I'm sending out obvious signals, and they switch at just the right time.

"I wanted to make this nice for your first time, but you decided against that, kitten. You only get to come if you ask nicely."

I glare at him. Jayden laughs. Cole pulls out enough for me to growl, "Fuck you." He shoves back in while Jayden is at my pussy again, lightly playing with it while stroking, not enough to get me off.

Cole pounds into my mouth and then yanks out, coming on my face and tits. Jayden also grunts and buries deep inside me. I feel him pulsing.

"Jesus, pull out." I kick at him.

He gives me a dark look and stays where he is. His voice is full of quiet warning. "Who do you belong to?"

A fog of pleasure and frustration fills me. "No one." I let my head drop back on the bed. They can take over my body, making it feel things I don't want to feel. But they can't have my mind.

"False," Cole growls. He rubs his fingers through his cum and sticks them in my mouth. He shoves them down my throat. "Us. You're ours. You wear our mark and our cum." I gag. He doesn't let up until he feels my tongue on his fingers, trying to push him out but also cleaning him off.

Jayden gets up and stands over me. "We'll have every part of you. Even that rebellious spirit you try to keep locked away. You're ours, kitten." He leans down and gives me a light kiss on the forehead. Cole follows suit. "And there's nothing you can do to stop it."

He stands up and throws on a shirt.

I look at the ripped pieces of my own shirt and glare. "I only have one left. Thanks a lot." I rub my thighs together.

Jayden cocks an eyebrow. "Well, let's go get you more. And if you touch yourself before you beg for my dick, I won't feed Sage."

My nostrils flare. "You wouldn't dare."

He shrugs. "Try me."

I throw myself out of Jayden's bed and start sliding on my pants before it registers. Wait. Did he say to go shopping? I snap my gaze between the two of them. Cole looks equally surprised.

Jayden is finishing up dressing and casually throws on a pair of shoes.

"Like, shopping?"

"Yeah." He's slipping on a pair of shoes.

"And I can go?"

He sighs. "They're for *you*."

I look around and then back at him. He looks like he's being serious. He'd risk that?

He opens the closet, and I hear beeping before he tucks something in his pants. A Glock. "This isn't a chance for you to run, kitten. Throw a shirt on."

I jump to obey. I keep thinking he'll say psych and punish me for wanting to go, but we walk to the front door. He sees I don't have shoes and heads back upstairs. He comes down with a pair of slides that are way too big for me, but I'm not complaining. I keep glancing at his face. It's impassive, as always.

"Is this another test?" I ask as I get into the back seat of the truck. Cole slides in next to me. He's also tucked a gun into his waistband.

"Not unless you make it one, kitten."

He starts the car. I let his asshole behavior go for a minute, and excitement floods my veins. I'm leaving! And I'm not being drug out. I'm going to see other people for the first time in... forever. My eyes tear up. For a second, I feel real gratitude toward Jayden for letting me get out. Then I realized how fucked up that is.

We roll out of the driveway. Other people. Real life. They can help me. I just have to get a message to them or get away from them long enough. I run through options in my head as we drive down the dirt driveway and turn right onto a paved road. It's just forest and hills around us now. I can use the bathroom and talk to someone in there. Maybe I can even grab one of their guns. Would I be able to shoot them?

I look between both of them. At first, I would have said yes all day long. Would have killed them without a second thought. And I hate that there's any hesitation right now. Of course, they deserve to die. They're going to hurt Sage. They have hurt Sage.

But not me. At least not in the way they've hurt her. My heart grows somber.

The clock on the dash says six thirty.

Jayden sees me glance at the clock in the rear-view mirror. "Want to pass the time, kitten? I seem to remember you didn't come."

Cole slides closer to me. He winks at me before sliding his hand over my hip and between my pants and skin. I don't stop him. I know it's useless to try, and he'll get off if I do. He starts circling my clit in gentle motions. He and Jayden start up a conversation about the weather and how we're supposed to get more snow.

Soon, I'm looking out the window and biting my lip, trying to ignore both of them. I'm already worked up, and Cole makes me feel good. So much better than anyone else has been able to do besides Jayden. But he doesn't let me come. I didn't think he would. He continues teasing me until we start to get into a more populated area. Until now, there's only been the occasional mailbox and driveway.

I sit up straighter and watch houses roll by. We roll up to a stop light, and Cole pinches my clit. I jump, worked up and horny. He leans into my neck. "No running, little one. As much as I would enjoy chasing you down, I don't think the woman in that car ahead of us would enjoy a bullet in the brain because she witnessed it."

He kisses my neck and leans back, rubbing again. I shiver and look at the car ahead of us. It's dark out, but I can see it's a maroon SUV with some sort of decal in the back window. He wouldn't hurt her...would he?

I put my hand on Cole's wrist to try and get him away from me. I glance up at him. He's looking at me. His face is serious.

I turn away. I'm overstimulated and jumpy. But I know if I tell him to stop, he'll do it even more. I sit quietly until we pull into the Walmart parking lot.

"I know you heard what Cole said." Jayden turns to look at me. "If you try to get help, if you try to pass a message, that person is going to die. We'll make it quiet and discrete. Think about how easily we picked up you and Sage. Don't make these innocent people have the same fate."

I swallow. Cole finally takes his hand out of my pants and jumps out of the car. He offers it to me like a gentleman. I don't take it and jump out. He grabs my hand and pulls me to him, kissing my forehead. To all the world, looking like a couple of people in love. He doesn't let go of my hand.

People hurry through the parking lot to get out of the cold. It feels odd to be back in society. I realize that real life has continued on without me. Was anyone even looking for me? I know Kyle and Carissa are. They would have raised hell, blasting my face all over social media. Would my followers be looking for me, too?

They walk me to the women's section of the store. I look around half-heartedly. "I don't have any money," I mutter.

Jayden gives me a look. "I'm buying. Get what you need."

I pick out some warm sweaters that look like they'll be hard to rip and some cheap shirts. I throw a pair of shoes on the pile that Jayden is carrying, and he doesn't say anything. I toss some warm socks on, too. As I'm looking at some panties since I'm tired of only having a few pairs, an old woman with a Walmart vest bustles up and starts stocking the shelves near me.

"Can I help you with anything?" She smiles at me.

I freeze. Her old eyes look so kind. Like she would help me. I flick my glance at the two men a few feet away. They're watching me. Jayden raises an eyebrow.

"No. Thanks."

"Alright." She keeps stocking the shelves.

I grab whatever panties were in front of me and throw them at Jayden. I can't even look at them. This is so fucked up. I didn't pick out a coat, but I'm over it. "Let's go," I mutter.

They guide me up to the self-checkout.

"Hey, momma," a man's voice slurs.

I look around. The guy in his early 40s in the checkout next to us is looking at me. His eyes are glossy, but he's dressed in a nice pair of jeans and a plaid shirt.

Cole steps between us and grabs my hand again.

"Wow, rude," he grumbles. "I was just trying to say hi. I

didn't mean anything by it." The man finishes checking out and mutters under his breath as he leaves.

I glare at Cole, but he isn't looking at me. He's staring at where the man walked out. Jayden finishes, and we also walk out. A blast of cold air takes my breath away. I'm walking slightly behind the men, trying to cling to the warmth a minute longer.

Suddenly, a hand squeezes my shoulder. I turn to see the man again. He must have waited for us to walk out. "You okay, baby?" His grip is harsh, and his strong cologne fills my nose. "I can treat a pretty thing like you better than that asshole."

I'm ripped away, and before I can process it, all I see is Jayden's black shirt. He speed-walks me back to the truck and practically tosses me and my clothes in. He starts the truck and takes off.

"Wait," I look out the back. He left Cole. We tear out of the lot.

I look at Jayden. There's a level of anger on his face that scares me. He looks ready to kill. We fly down the road. I notice a small sedan with dim lights right behind us. Did he think I tried to pass a message to the man?

I shake. This is it. This is where they hurt me.

"Did he hurt you?" The words come through his gritted teeth.

"What? No."

He drives in charged silence. I see the vein on his neck pulsing. We get into the wooded area again. I turn around and see the same dim headlights.

Suddenly, Jayden whips the car to the side of the road. I scramble to stay sitting up. He gets out of the truck and slams the door closed.

I also get out, seeing that the other car has stopped behind us. Cole steps out of the passenger side. He has the man from the store at gunpoint. Jayden rips the driver's door open and yanks the man out like he weighs nothing.

"What the hell! I didn't do nothing." The man's hands are in front of his face, and he tries to back away. With one hand, Jayden throws him into the hood of the car and leans into him. "How *dare* you touch our woman."

His voice vibrates in the dark, angry and low.

"What? I didn't know!" The man glances at me, then between the two men. Cole has a wicked grin on his face.

"If you want the car, take it. I swear to God I didn't know."

Almost faster than I can register, Jayden punches him in the face. The man crumples.

"Think you can put your filthy hands on something that doesn't belong to you?" Jayden punches him again. The man cries out.

Cole laughs.

"Stop!" I step forward, but Jayden doesn't even turn around.

"You don't even deserve to breathe the same air as her." He punches him again.

I grab his arm and hold it as tight as I can. "Fucking stop! He didn't do anything!"

Cole snatches me off Jayden and pulls me back. Jayden continues to punch him in his torso, back, and head. All because of me. Because he was in the wrong place at the wrong time.

I tremble in rage and scratch and swipe at Cole. He picks me up and throws me into the back of the truck.

"Stay, little one. Or we'll kill him. He's lucky we aren't." He slams the door so hard that the cab shakes. I scramble to the window. The man isn't fighting anymore, just curled up on the hood of the car. Something in Cole's hand glints in the light. A knife. Jayden moves aside, and Cole snatches up the man's hand. There's a flash and a scream, and I see blood on the man's hand in a long gash across his palm.

The voices are muted. "If you breathe a word of this to anyone, we'll kill you, Mr. Joe Robinson of...214 Main Avenue." Cole slaps something into the man's hand on top of the gash. A driver's license. "As far as you're concerned, you lost a bar fight, yeah?"

The man nods his head, his whole body shaking. I make out him saying, "I didn't know, I'm sorry. I'm sorry. I have a wife and a dog; please don't kill me."

Cole slaps his back like they're friends. "What bar were you at?"

"T-The Rainbow."

"What happened?"

"Got in a f-fight."

"Good. Now get out of here."

He scrambles into his car, and it peels off. I'm shaking. My vision is tunneled on the two men. They wait until he's driven off and then get back in the truck.

I stare blankly ahead. My body is strangely still and emotionless. "You are monsters."

Cole throws me a blinding grin. Jayden doesn't look at me.

"God, I'm hungry." Cole looks into my eyes, and then his gaze dips down to my crotch.

Anger fills past the fog, and I seethe, "No." How could he be horny right now? Cole turns on the radio and kicks his feet back into the dash. He flicks his knife around in his fingers.

"You can't do this." My voice is droll, "We can't keep living in this...bubble. I have a boyfriend. A life. A house and a car. I have a life. You have to let me go."

The car goes silent except for the radio. I feel the energy shift. Fear spikes through me.

"Man, I thought she had more sense than that." Cole looks to Jayden.

Jayden cuts a glance back to me. "If you want that piece of shit to keep breathing, you'll stop talking about him. He doesn't deserve your attention."

Who, Kyle? "No! You can't just threaten everyone around me!"

"Yes. I can."

"You're going to get caught! You can't keep getting away with this. Your luck will run out, and you'll get caught."

"Will I?" He looks at me. There is no emotion in his gaze.

"Yes," I hiss.

"Hmmm." He leans back and keeps driving. When we get back, I run to the shower again. It's become my safe space. I shower and plan and think about the dangerous men and how, like it or not, they've become a part of my life.

FOR THE NEXT FEW WEEKS, I listen to them detox Sage, only to force her to get high again. Over and over. It's excruciating. She won't talk to me. They won't talk to me about her.

They edge me constantly. They fuck me separately and together but don't try anything they haven't already done. They refuse to let me come unless I beg, and I'd rather die than let them make me beg to come. It's like I've made this my last line in the sand. Like I can't be guilty of any of this, I can't enjoy their presence, I can't be held responsible if I don't allow myself to come.

They even shower with me to make sure I don't play with myself when they're not around. I feel like I'm going crazy. I've never been more turned on in my life. It feels like I'm hitting puberty all over again, except multiplied by ten. I'm pretty sure I've come from my dreams, but when I wake up to chase that high, they stop me, fuck me, and put me to bed wet. They've always been attractive to me, but now my cunt wants to jump all over them every time I see them.

One afternoon, Jayden tosses me a jacket. "I'm going out on the ATV. Want to ride?"

"Sure." I jump up from the couch. We fixed it a few days ago. I feel like if I sit in his cabin any longer, I'll go crazy.

We walk outside, and the day is much warmer than it usually is. It snowed the day before, but it's starting to melt. The sun even peeks through the clouds. Jayden has already pulled the bike out of the garage. He hops on, leaving me to slide on behind him. I glower about it. As soon as I'm on, he hits the throttle, the lurch forcing me to grab his torso. I feel his chuckle.

We drive down the driveway. We don't talk over the sound of the engine. I just watch the trees go by and feel Jayden's warmth soak into me. I can feel his abs through his hoodie. He flexes every time he turns the bike. The intimate position has blood flowing to my pussy.

At the end of the driveway, he turns left. I perk up.

Jayden doesn't seem concerned, which tells me no cars will probably drive by. We drive for a bit, seeing rabbits and squirrels startle away at our sound.

A grown-over dirt driveway appears on our left, and Jayden turns into it. There's an old mailbox as well. We pull up to a clearing and an old, two-story cabin. It's clear it's abandoned, with the front door standing open and no glass in half of the windows. Jayden stops the bike.

"Where are we?"

Jayden gets off and turns to me. "One of my favorite places to come with Cole as a teen."

"You knew him when you were teenagers?"

He grunts and starts towards the house. I get off the bike and follow him up the steps. They wobble as we walk.

"This doesn't seem safe."

He laughs, "It's not." He throws a devilish look over his shoulder. "But I'll protect you."

"Jesus." I glare at him, but he's already walked inside. I follow. It takes my eyes a second to adjust. The inside is just as run down as the rest of it. It looks like whoever used to live here just left all their things and trash behind too.

"We own the place now." Jayden looks back.

I cross my arms. "I thought cops didn't make a lot of money." I know this place is junk, but land is so expensive.

He laughs and reaches out a hand. "I'm not a cop anymore. And Cole's family has a lot of money."

I don't take his hand. "I thought he said they grew up poor."

"They did. That's why his mom married his stepdad when we were teens." He starts up the steps. They're dingy and lean a little toward the right.

I follow. If they can hold his big-ass body, they can hold me. He leads me to the end of the only room upstairs, toward a window that faces the front of the cabin. The ceilings are slanted in with the roof, and he has to walk in the middle to avoid bending down. This area is a lot more cleared out than the others, with a space heater and other junk pushed against one wall. The window is open, and under it sits a bag of bird food.

Something skitters in the hallway, and I jump. Jayden smirks, throwing out a handful of food on the window ledge and some in the room as well. He snaps out two camping chairs and motions for me to sit.

"You feeding all the rodents in here as well?" I move stiffly next to him and sit.

"Just cause they're ugly doesn't mean they don't deserve to eat."

He sits quietly, looking out the window. We sit like that for a while, watching the wind move the bare trees outside. The sun glints off the ATV in the yard.

I break the silence. "Why did you become a cop?"

He lifts his lip in a half smile like he's amused by the question. He looks so beautiful when he smiles.

"I don't know. I was young and wanted to save the world. I didn't realize that saving the world still doesn't help you save yourself."

I glare at the floor.

"Why did you become an influencer?" His voice sounds bigger in the small room.

"For fun." I wrap my arms around my legs against a breeze that comes through the window. He glances at me.

"It gets cold in here, but the birds don't mind."

At that moment, a finch lands on the windowsill, its wings and the scrape of its feet loud. Jayden sees my small jump and chuckles quietly. "Easy kitten. No one's going to hurt you."

The bird seems unconcerned with us being there and pecks away.

"You already have," I mutter under my breath.

The mood grows dark. The bird flies away, and I grow uncomfortable with the silence. I ask, "Why'd you leave? Being a cop."

He looks at me again. He pulls a cigarette out of his pocket and lights it up. He takes a long draw, then hands it to me.

I wave him off.

He exhales the cloud of smoke, blowing it away from me, and finally answers. "Got tired of all the bullshit. Tired of the hours. Tired of the people. Someone tried to kill me one night, and I shot him. That was the beginning of the end for me."

I stare at his side profile. He looks unaffected, pulling on the cigarette. I can't help myself; I look down at his waistband. He didn't bring the gun today. That I can see.

"Tell me," he says. "Why did you date Kyle?"

The room grows silent.

"What?" I sputter.

"You knew he could never make you happy. He bored you, even. And yet you stayed. Why?"

My mouth drops open. "I loved him!" I correct myself, "Love him."

His dark eyes flash to me. "Loved? Do you even know what love is?"

I cross my arms, anger flashing through me. "Do *you*?"

He takes another draw, letting the smoke out slowly. "No. I suppose I don't."

Another bird drops on the windowsill, pecking at the food and spreading it on the floor. We watch in silence.

Eventually, he speaks again. "He's not worth it, you know."

"Why? Because you're jealous?" I hold out my hand for the cigarette. It's almost done. He hands it to me. It's been a long time since I've smoked, but I need something.

"Just trust me."

I laugh, then cough around my lungful of smoke. I grind out the butt on the floor. "I don't think you need me to explain how rich that is coming from you."

He doesn't respond. I sit, tense. Eventually, when he doesn't ask any more questions, I relax. Birds swing by, eating at the food until all that's left are husks and sunflower seed shells.

Jayden stands. I follow him back out of the house and climb up behind him on the bike again. We go back to the cabin. Cole isn't there.

Jayden keeps the ATV keys on him and rearms the front door. "Changed the code, kitten. You'd make it thirty feet down the driveway before I'm balls deep in you."

I glare at him, and he flashes me a wink. He looks like Cole in that second. Then he heads upstairs.

I knock softly at Sage's door. As usual, she doesn't answer, so I go in. She's on the bed, curled on her side. She barely opens her eyes as I come in. I replace her water bottles with new ones and sit beside her. Her eyes are sunken in, and it looks like she's been crying.

When she speaks, it scares me. I haven't heard her talk in weeks.

"I liked all your videos, you know."

I stare at her.

She closes her eyes. "I'd never tried eggs in my ramen before you. Made Jayden try it too." She gives a sad smile.

"I, uh, thanks." I rub the back of my neck. I wince at how awkward I sound. I say in a softer tone, "For what it's worth, I'm sorry." I'm not sure what I'm apologizing for. All of it, maybe. That she even found me in the first place.

She closes her eyes and then opens them again. "It's not your fault. Jayden is a controlling asshole."

I look at my hands. I don't want to push her too much. "Why does he hate you so much? Did you break up with him?"

She sighs, "No, he broke up with me. We were...having a hard time. After the shooting, he wasn't the same, but it started before that too."

So they broke up recently. "I'm sorry." I pick at one of my nails.

"It's fine. I got mad...after he broke up with me. I..." she clears her throat and stares at the floor. For the first time, I see some color in her cheeks. "I wanted him to see what he lost...make him realize he should have treated me better. So I..."

She pauses for a long time.

"You...what?"

She gets angry and bites out, "I...hooked up with Pat." She sneers. "His stepdad."

I blink.

"Yeah, yeah, I don't want to hear it." She glares at the wall.

I sit in stunned silence.

Her voice drops low. "I didn't know about him. I swear I didn't. Not until it was too late."

I don't like the tone of her voice. I look at her. "Know about...what?"

She looks at me. The anger is gone like it was never there and there is hardly any life left in her eyes. She looks a hundred years old. "That he is...was, a pedophile."

I get a sinking feeling in my gut. She closes her eyes slowly. We sit like that for a little. She finally says, "I swear I had no idea. Jayden never told me about what he did to him and Cole."

I feel sick. Nausea rolls over my body, and I get hot.

"I'm tired," she says suddenly. "I'd like to sleep."

I clear my throat. "Sure, yeah." I stand up.

She closes her eyes. "Sleep and never wake up."

My gut is churning. I close her door and stare at the wood. I spend a few hours in the living room, turning my awkward wooden ice cream creation around and around in my hands as my thoughts churn and my stomach hurts.

Finally, I walk up to the loft. Jayden is reading on the bed. He smiles when he sees me. "Kitten. You ready to beg?"

Heat flares in me, but I cross my arms. "Sage is breaking. Past the point of return."

He shuts his book and gives me a serious look. "You need to stop thinking about her. She's none of your concern."

"She's a human being."

That doesn't seem to affect him.

"Whatever she's done in the past..." I grow increasingly uncomfortable. "I'm sorry about what happened."

I can feel his gaze on me, but I don't look at him. I can't.

"Are you now?"

"Yes. And I'm sorry I kissed Sage. I didn't know. She didn't know!" Emotions flush through my cheeks.

"I'm not sorry. I wouldn't have gotten you."

Slowly, I look at him. He looks possessive. I feel my anger rise. "Letting her die won't solve anything now."

He blinks at me. Then he says, very slowly. "Sage killed my mother, Jo."

The world seems to slow. I stare at him, trying to read him. For once, he doesn't shutter his gaze. I see pain. Deep sadness that can't be faked. It floods his black eyes until there's nothing left. And then, in an instant, he hardens them again. He grabs my wrist. "So no, kitten. It won't solve anything now. But I don't care."

He pulls me to him and jerks so I fall on top of him. Too quick for me to fight, he flips me over so he's lying on top of me.

"Jayden..."

He locks eyes with me, his voice stern. "What do you call me?"

I freeze. His dark eyes pierce mine, seeming to see all the way into me. I try to get away, but he has me pinned.

"I don't..."

"Sir," he reminds.

The pressure of his body sends sparks of pleasure down to my cunt. Despite everything, I feel myself getting wet. "Sir."

"Good girl." He puts his nose to the top of my breasts and breathes in. I feel my nipples pebble.

He notices. He gives me a look, and his eyes glitter. "You must need to come so bad. I've been waiting all day for you to come crawling to me."

I glare at him. "You're the one that threw me on the bed like a caveman."

He grins, slowly licking his bottom lip. I feel him settle between my hips.

"Do you want this dick?" He shifts again, and the movement causes pleasure to zip up my clit. I swallow. I do want it.

He can tell. He fists my hair and yanks just hard enough to hurt. He growls, "Beg."

I groan. I don't want to lose. I've been fighting him on this for weeks.

"Fucking beg." His voice doesn't sound nice. There's a warning in it. "I already own your soul. Stop fighting me."

"Never," I whisper.

He yanks on my hair again, sending pain shooting down my skull. It only turns me on more.

"If I have to fight you for the rest of our lives, I'll do it." His mouth is close to my ear, and his breath is hot. "I love it when you fight me, kitten. Your hatred gives me life. So, if you want to come, you'll beg for it."

I dig my fingers into his skin. He doesn't even flinch away. I keep scratching into him, and he bites at my neck, my shoulders, and my tits as I scratch and scratch. I'm writing a word with my marks.

He rips my clothes off. "That's fine," he growls. "If you don't want to come, I still will."

I grip his shirt and work to yank it over his head. He grabs my cunt.

I smirk. He pauses and looks down. He freezes, and then his eyes lock with mine.

I've scratched a crude 'please' into his torso.

Jayden tears into me, crashing his mouth down on mine with feral energy, eating and licking and sucking with fervent energy. It's all I can do to keep up with him. He plays with my pussy as he does. I'm already so worked up that I feel myself coming to the edge of an orgasm.

"Come, my pretty, naughty woman," Jayden growls in my ear.

I do. Pleasure fills me, and my cunt pulses around nothing. I don't even come down off my orgasm before he's filling me. I gasp at the pressure. He's big.

"Good girl," he mutters. "Good fucking girl."

I rake my nails down his back hard enough to earn a hiss of pain from him. He pulls out of me and flips me over so I'm on my stomach.

"Play with yourself," he demands.

I do, rubbing my hard clit. It doesn't take long before I'm coming around his cock. It feels electrifying. Lights flash behind my eyes.

He grunts. I keep rubbing, chasing a follow-up orgasm. Jayden wraps his hand around my throat and squeezes. "What a nasty girl."

The next orgasm hits quick and hard. Jayden slams even harder into me, barely letting up on my neck. I feel his teeth on my shoulder, biting hard. He bites so hard I wiggle to get away.

He releases his teeth. "That's right. Try to run. It won't do you any good." He bites me again viciously. I cry out. He continues biting me while slamming his dick into me. It's violent and brutal and hot.

When I come again, it's a mix of pleasure and pain as he bites into my ass. He's biting so hard I'm sure it'll leave marks.

He wrings orgasm after orgasm out of me. I get sensitive, and the orgasms begin hurting, but he doesn't stop.

"You asked to come, kitten," he says with an evil tone. He moves over me, sweaty abs glistening, making me want to lick all the way up his scratched torso.

Finally, when I truly don't think I can come again, he shudders and comes. We both collapse on the bed, breathing heavily. After weeks of edging, those orgasms were more powerful than I'd ever felt. I think about getting up to use the bathroom, then close my eyes, just for a second.

# COLE

## 29

OUR GIRL IS ASLEEP UPSTAIRS. JAYDEN FUCKED THE absolute shit out of her. Used her and marked her pretty pale skin. Made her come until she passed out. I can't wait for her to wake up so I can do the same.

We sit in the kitchen, and Jayden stuffs his face. I pull out my phone and slide it to him.

"What's this?" He looks at it.

I point to the most recent call. "Captain Flynn. He called me wanting to know where you were."

Jayden stills. "The fuck?"

"He's still sniffing around for Sage."

He looks at me. He stops eating.

"We need to move on that. She's starting to put us in danger."

Jayden runs a hand over his face.

"The last thing we want is a search warrant, and they find her here. She'll talk about Pat."

"They can't." Jayden shoves his plate away. "They don't have shit."

"That you *know* of. People pay attention to missing women's stories. You have luck, but this is the third time someone related to you has disappeared, Jayden. You know as well as I do the cops are sniffing up your ass right now."

He sighs and glances towards the loft. "Anything new for her?"

"Not since I last updated you." I've been keeping a close eye on the chatter surrounding Jo's disappearance. Her best friend has started causing problems but has shifted a lot of the suspicion to Kyle, and that's what the keyboard warriors are focused on at the moment.

He sighs in relief. "Okay. We'll do it tonight. Our old spot."

I nod. Good. Maybe I can still get my dick wet before we go.

## 30

I'm sore, but Cole fucks me thoroughly as soon as I wake up. I thought I was done coming after Jayden, but I was very wrong. My body responds to Cole with hunger and lust.

I drag myself down to the shower, feeling fully used. When I come out, I pad up the stairs. I hear the men talking.

"We need to take her with us." It's Jayden.

"She won't like it."

I freeze on the steps. I'm not far enough up that they can see me yet.

"She's already escaped us once, and she's smart. It's been weeks since she last tried. Something is cooking, and I don't trust her enough to leave her."

Cole sounds frustrated. "Then dope her up and throw her in the back of the truck. You're going to traumatize her."

My stomach cramps.

There's silence. Then, "I won't hide who I am from her. She's going to find out sooner or later. She deserves to know."

My heart races, and I shudder in a breath.

"Jesus, okay. But you gonna patch me up after she tries to kill me?"

"You get off on that, don't even try."

There's a dark laugh.

I feel sick. I kick myself for growing complacent. Of course, something bad is going to happen. They beat a man for touching me; these men who I've been having mind-blowing sex with aren't good men. My hands and feet feel numb, and my vision is tunneled. I try to back down the steps and trip over my feet.

"Little one," Cole's voice sounds behind me. I jump and turn. My eyes feel wide.

If he didn't suspect me before, he does now. He drops the act and narrows his eyes. "Were you spying on us, lemon drop?"

I swallow. He has cargo pants and black boots on.

"No. I'm getting cramps. I was going to grab a pad." I start to go back down the stairs. If I can get to his room, I can get a knife.

"Get your shoes." His voice barks in command. "We're going out."

I keep going. "Hang on, I'll be right there."

I hear footsteps, and his hand grips my shoulder. He turns me around, making my back bump into the wall. I try to get my adrenaline under control. I raise my chin.

For a split second, his gaze softens, but then it's gone, and he looks dangerous again. "Now, little one."

Fine. I stalk past him. He follows closely, within arms reach. I look around wildly, but there's nothing within my reach that I can sneak. He's hovering too closely. I grab my shoes and put them on slowly. I then look for my sweater.

"Procrastinating won't make it go away." His voice is softer, almost kind.

I glare at him.

His gaze doesn't waver. He takes me down to the truck and sits beside me in the back seat. I'm fully shaking now. And that makes me angry.

Cole rubs my thigh. "He's not going to hurt you, little one."

I whip my head around and stare at his hand. The same hand

that made me come just a little bit ago. I snap my gaze up to his. "Why do I need to be drugged for this, Cole? And my name is Jo."

There's hardness in his eyes. "Why do you care about her so much?"

"What?" My mouth drops open.

"Sage. You don't even know her."

"I don't need to know her to know you shouldn't hurt her."

"I won't. Jayden will."

I rear back.

"But that's beside the point." He leans into me. "Why. Do. You. Care?" His gaze searches mine.

I look away.

"It's not your fault." Cole gently grabs my chin. He moves it, so I'm looking at him again. I close my eyes.

"Hey." He flicks my nose, and I open my eyes in surprise. "This is on Jayden. Not you."

"Fuck you," I snarl. "Let me go. Just let me go."

He leans back, and the wall falls fully in front of his eyes. "Strap in."

I think about clawing my way out of the car. Cole doesn't wait. He pushes me back into the seat, reaches across me, and straps me in. He sits so close to me that his thigh presses into mine. I stare straight ahead.

Something thumps in the back of the truck, and then Jayden gets into the driver's seat. I barely glance at him, just staring at the headrest of the seat in front of me.

## 31

I'VE BEEN AVOIDING THIS. NOT BECAUSE I'M AFRAID TO KILL or because I have feelings for Sage. Those parts of my soul died a long time ago. But because I hate to acknowledge that deep, gut-wrenching loss again. It's always there, but recently it's eased. Just being around Jo has calmed my soul, and I keep avoiding ruining that. Grasping onto that small level of peace like it'll save me. I knew I should have acted when I had that nightmare in front of her. Instead, I just sank further into her, pretending like she, Cole, and I were the only ones to exist.

But it's time. I've started to put her in jeopardy of being found by the cops. Even the thought sends me into a rage toward myself and the cops. I put her in this spot. And I don't like to admit that it scares me.

I drive them to the abandoned house. It's where Cole and I killed Pat, so it's only fitting. Our kitten sits quietly in the back seat. She stares at nothing, her hands clasped in her lap.

I recognize that look. Cole and I had it many times when we were young. It sends a pang of pain through me, immediately followed by anger and helplessness.

I slam my door and wrench hers open. She jumps a little. I

unstrap her, grab her by her neck, and yank her out of the car. She gasps as I slam her into the side of the truck.

She looks at me. I give her a mocking smile.

Her blue eyes flare with hate.

Good. There she is again. She needs to hold onto something, and if it's hate, so be it. I smirk and shove her toward the house. Cole follows behind her. He knows where to take her.

Sage is still bound in the back of my truck. I put a coat and pants on her and bound her with scarves so she wouldn't have rub marks on her wrists and ankles. Just in case the cops find her before her body gets beyond recognition.

Sage gives me a terrified look. It makes me angry. All I see when I look at her is the texts between her and my mother. Grief hits me in the gut. Was my mother afraid when she realized she couldn't breathe?

I throw her over my shoulder and march inside.

It's darker here, and I have to blink to adjust. We go past the stairs and to the run-down living room. Cole has Jo on one of the folding chairs. She's seething. I grab ahold of her anger like it's a tangible thing and let it wash over my sadness.

I set Sage down on the couch gently. Not because I care how she feels. But I don't want to leave any bruises on her body. What cushions the couch does have are wrapped in black trash bags that are ripped in various places. Sage struggles to get away, but she's weak and dope sick.

"It's time, Sage."

She spits at me. It lands on the floor by my boot. I look at it, putting on a bored expression. Movement catches my eye, and I see the fire in Jo. Good. Part of me hates myself for putting her through this. I shove that feeling away.

I reach into my pocket and pull out a baggie. Inside are pills. I shake them in Sage's face.

"Fuck you," she growls. But I can see she wants them. Needs them.

I kneel down to her level and lean into her. Over her shoulder, I make eye contact with Jo. I speak low. "This is the exact same amount you gave my mother." Jo's eyebrows raise. Despite my efforts, my chest hurts.

I sense that Sage has gone incredibly still.

I keep looking at Jo. "I've built back up your tolerance. Who knows. Maybe it won't kill you."

Sage shudders. I see Jo battle against herself. She can't decide whether to fight or shut down. I wink at her. She stiffens.

I turn back to Sage. "My mom was clean. For the first time in her life, she was clean. And you ruined that." Pain wraps my heart in searing heat.

All the fight leaves Sage. It disgusts me. I toss a water bottle at her. "You'll swallow all of them. You can thank me. If I made you snort them, you'd definitely die."

"Please, don't do this," she sobs weakly. The weakness makes rage fill me.

"Wasn't fucking step-daddy enough? What, I didn't pay enough attention to you, so you had to go after my mom too? And then, *then*. You text my *dead* mother a video of you kissing another girl to make me jealous because you know I have her phone. There was no 'please' then."

All of the emotions that I try to keep buried down are boiling. I have to look at the wall. I see Cole looking at me. He's sad. We lock eyes and hold. Then I look at my little kitten. There's a war of emotions in her eyes. I see pity.

That tips me over the edge. I don't need pity. I snatch up Sage's hair and tilt her head back. "Take the pills, or I'll force them down your throat," I hiss.

She struggles weakly.

"Fine." I snatch up the bag.

"No!" Jo jumps up from the chair, but Cole grabs her around the waist, dragging her back against his body. She's fully lost it, struggling and fighting and tearing. She looks like a wild animal.

Her panic tugs at me. I hate seeing her like that. Afraid, yes. But not so far gone she loses herself, and I hate that she's affecting me.

I grip Sage's jaw in anger and force her mouth open.

"Stop. Jayden, please. Please stop."

I look up. Jo has torment all over her face. She's fighting. It feels like the world slows. For a second, I think about listening to the girl who took my life by storm. The girl whose sass and fight and hate have breathed life into my dead soul. I actually think about giving up my revenge. I shake myself. This plan was the only thing that pulled me out of my depressive slump. The only thing I thought about every night...until I saw Jo's beautiful face in that video. This and Cole were the only thing that kept me out of an early grave. But Sage knows about Pat. And if she told, the cops would take me and Cole away from my kitten. She can't live.

I look at Cole. "Shut her up."

He wraps his hand around Jo's mouth. I force the pills into Sage's mouth and clasp my hand over her mouth and nose. She fights and struggles for so long that I think she'll pass out. Finally, I feel her struggle to swallow. She chokes on the amount and the dry swallowing. I don't care.

Once I make sure she's swallowed them all, I drop her back on the couch. I stand over her so she can't vomit them up again. I wait until she droops and then wait some more. It takes forever. She passes out, her breathing slow. I drop the empty baggie near her hand. My mom had to die alone. So will Sage. I'll deal with her body later.

It's only then that I look at Jo. I expect hate, anger, horror. I see nothing. She looks at me blankly. It's a thousand-yard stare.

"Let's go." I motion for Cole to follow.

He releases Jo, and she continues to show no emotion. She just follows like an obedient dog.

And somehow, that hurts more.

# COLE

## 32

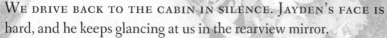

WE DRIVE BACK TO THE CABIN IN SILENCE. JAYDEN'S FACE IS hard, and he keeps glancing at us in the rearview mirror.

Jo says nothing. She does whatever I tell her to do, but there's nothing in her eyes. I've seen dissociation before. I don't try to break her from it. When we get back, I carry her upstairs and lay her in our bed. I go downstairs and glare at Jayden.

"I told you she didn't need to see that."

He throws me an angry look. "She'll be fine."

"Sure. She'll be fine in the way we're fine." Anger rolls through me, and I snatch up a whittling piece I'd been working on. It's starting to look like Jo on her knees – naked. The knife gives me the tiniest amount of peace, but I want to cut skin with it. Draw blood.

I glance at Jayden and can tell he's deeply angry. "I said she's fine."

"Whatever, man." I pick and chop and slice with no finesse.

"Listen, I was going to chase Sage through the house before I did it. Maybe scare her and make her pay. But I didn't."

"I said whatever."

There's a soft moan upstairs, and we both pause. It sounded like she was in pain.

"Did you leave anything up there?" Jayden snaps.

"No."

Jo moans again, followed by the sounds of retching. This time, there's no mistaking the pain. Both of us go upstairs. She's lying on the edge of the bed, gripping her stomach. She pukes on the floor.

I grab the trash can and put it by the bed. She's violently shaking. I sit next to her.

"She's just in shock," Jayden says.

"Hey." I grab her shoulder. She continues to shake. She squints her eyes closed like she's in pain. "Hey, little one."

She doesn't respond. Instead, she leans over and pukes again.

"It's just your body reacting to stress. Let it out." Jayden crosses his arms, but a flash of guilt comes across his face.

She grits her teeth and lets out a deep moan.

"What's going on, little one?"

She opens her eyes and looks around in a panic. She's still not there. It looks like she's looking right through us. She breathes heavily while her teeth chatter. "Oh my god, it hurts."

"Jay, something's not right." I look her over. I don't see anything wrong.

He gets down on her other side and starts to pat her down.

She screams, gaze bouncing between us. She scrambles to get back, then doubles over again, puking on the bed.

"Fuck." Jayden lifts up her shirt. Everything looks fine.

"Jayden," I bark and move her leg off where she was sitting before. The bed is smeared in blood.

"Fuck!" He pats her down aggressively, looking for hidden weapons. There's nothing.

"Did she take something?"

"There's nothing to take. All the meds are locked up."

We strip her of her clothes, and it's then we discover the blood is coming from her pelvis. She fights us, and then her body locks up in pain again and again.

"Some women get terrible periods. How are hers?" I hold her hair back as she dry heaves.

Jayden runs a hand through his hair. "I don't know."

"What do you mean you don't know?" I snap.

"She hasn't had one. Not a real one, anyway."

I lock my gaze with his. We are still for a second. "How long has she been here, Jay?"

He calculates. "Fuck." He runs his hand through his hair again and starts pacing.

We stay in silence for a little until her pained moan comes again. I grab her up and walk her to the shower, where I turn it on as hot as I can get it. I carry her in. My clothes get soaked under the spray, and she curls into me. The shaking doesn't stop. Every few minutes, she grabs at me, groaning. There's a steady stream of red down the shower drain.

Instead of getting better, her moans start turning to screams. Jayden followed us into the bathroom.

"Something is wrong, Jay." I can't help the slight fear in my voice. "I don't know what to do for this."

He throws this phone down on the sink. "I know. It's too much blood."

We don't say anything for a bit.

"I think we need to get her to the hospital."

Jayden grimaces. He looks conflicted. I also feel torn. I don't want to lose her. She tenses and screams again.

Finally, he nods.

# Mary Jo

## 33

I'M NOT SURE WHAT'S GOING ON. PAIN LIKE I'VE NEVER FELT before rips through my stomach. There are voices around me. They sound familiar, but I'm not sure why.

The fog clears for a second. I'm in a car, lying on my side. My head is on someone's legs.

"Hurry." The voice is familiar. Cole?

The motion of the car makes me sick. I dry heave onto the floor. I close my eyes again as another wave of pain rips into me. I let the fog take over again.

~

WHEN I OPEN my eyes again, I don't recognize where I am. There's a white wall with some kind of diagram on it. There's a curtain hanging from the ceiling. I look around. Jayden is slumped over in a chair. I have an I.V. in my hand. My heart races, and I start to gasp for breath.

Jayden starts awake. He immediately stands and grabs my hand. "Kitten. How are you?"

My voice is hoarse. "Where am I?"

"Hospital." He brushes some hair off my forehead. His eyes are...pained.

I remember the agonizing pain. I still feel it, but it's muted. "What happened?"

He winces just the slightest bit.

"Jayden?" I feel my stomach with my hands. "What happened?"

He looks down at my hand. He traces little circles on my skin. "The doctor will come in and tell you."

"No." I grip his hand, making him look at me. Fear is pounding in my blood. "What. Happened?"

"You had a miscarriage."

The world slows to a stop. Sounds mute, and everything except him fades. Finally, I get a word out. "What?"

He just keeps tracing circles on my hand. I blink. A miscarriage? You have to be pregnant to have those. I wasn't...

Jayden presses into my side. He moves my hand over his waistband. "I'm sorry, kitten." There's raw agony in his voice. "I'm really sorry. But I won't lose you."

"What?" His tone scares me. I try to pull my hand away. He presses it into something hard and metal under his shirt. Does he have a gun?

There's a knock at the door.

"If you try to pass a message on, I'll kill them. Don't talk to any of the nurses. Don't talk to any of the staff."

I look up at him in disbelief. He won't meet my gaze.

The door opens, and someone bustles past the curtain. It's a nurse. She smiles when she sees me up. "Mary, you're awake." She has brown hair and hearing aids, but she looks to be in her thirties. She goes to the computer and badges in. "You must have questions."

I blink. She talks to me about miscarriage and something about my cervix and abnormalities. It goes by in a blur. All I feel is Jayden by my side and a sense of spiraling. At some point, she leaves. Jayden grabs my hand and just holds it.

I don't look at him.

"Jo," he says.

"Where's Cole?"

"They won't let him in unless he's family."

I turn to look at him finally. His scruff is deeply shadowed, and there are dark circles under his eyes. His gaze looks more shuttered than normal.

"How are you here then?"

"I'm your husband."

Feeling breaks through the cloud I'm in. I snatch my hand back. "No, you're not."

There is no expression on his face, no spark behind his eyes.

Anger and disbelief build. I can't even process the...miscarriage. If that's even what happened. I don't even want to think about it. I always knew I wanted a kid, but it was always so far in the future.

I swallow. I feel like I'm in a dream. I want to go back to what I know. My first thought is the cabin, the big bed, and strong, warm bodies. Fuck. How could I think that? I want my bed. *My* bed. At home. Kyle.

Jayden is watching me. I drop my head in my hands. "Can I have a minute?"

He hesitates.

My voice comes out in a whisper, "Please."

He gets up. "I'll be right outside." He kisses the top of my head. His gun presses into my side, and he leaves.

A FEW HOURS LATER, they say something about infection and blood loss. I don't pay attention. Jayden leaves every two hours on the hour and is gone for about fifteen minutes. Sometimes, he comes back with food. He tells me Cole is outside waiting. I don't eat anything. I'm not hungry. I barely speak to the hospital staff. Jayden jumps up to help me anytime I say anything.

Finally, around dinner time and close to his two-hour break, I stretch. Jayden's gaze darts up. "I'm hungry," I say.

He gets up. "I'll get you something."

"I want McDonalds. Ten-piece chicken nuggets with a Sprite."

He starts texting on his phone. "I'll get Cole to get some."

"Thanks," I mutter.

He pauses and seems uncomfortable. I watch him. He fidgets and asks, "How are you?"

I shake my head. "I just want to get out of here. When can I go?"

"Hopefully tonight."

I let my head fall back on the pillow. "You stink. You need a shower."

A ghost of a smile traces his lips, followed by a look of pure pain. As soon as he notices me watching him, he masks all expressions.

In about ten minutes, Jayden leaves the room.

It's what I was waiting for. Now is my chance. I stare wearily at the wall. Run, run, run; it feels like all I do is run.

I swing both feet over the edge of the bed and start to pad to the door. I'm attached to an IV pole. I consider, then pull the IV out of my hand.

Jayden isn't outside. I move down the hall and find the nurses' station. I tell them my room and ask for my nurse. I should be anxious, but I don't feel anything. She shows up, looking me over. "You can't take out your I.V."

I motion her farther away from the nurse's station. She starts to try to herd me back to my room. For a moment, I consider letting her. I'm tired. So tired.

I plant my feet. "That is not my husband."

She turns back around. "What do you mean?"

I look around. "That man with me. He's not my husband." She looks back towards the room.

"I don't have a car or money, but I need to get away."

"You can't leave; you need more fluids and meds. You were in critical condition a few hours ago."

I can't get myself to care.

"Is he abusive?"

I hesitate. Not really. But also, yes. But I need her to believe that so I can get away. "Yes." My stomach sours, knowing that's what Sage said about him when she met me. Thinking about Sage makes me want to throw up. Is that going to happen to me once he figures out I've tried to run? The thought is almost enough to send me back to my room like nothing happened.

"Did he have anything to do with your miscarriage?"

"What? No." Well, yes. He got me pregnant in the first place. Or did Cole? I scrunch my eyes closed.

"Okay. We'll try to help you, honey. He won't be allowed back in the room."

"No." I bark, then run a hand through my hair. "Please, he'll hurt you if he knows I said anything. Don't call the cops. He's a cop, and they'll know where I am. Please, I just need to get out of here and get a ride."

She looks at me like she's trying to decide whether I'm telling the truth or not. Finally, she pats my arm. "My last husband was a piece of shit also. Stay here." She goes across to the nurse's station.

I wrap my arms around myself. I'm in one of their gowns with grippy socks. I wait and wait. It has to have been at least five minutes. I don't have much time.

For the first time, I feel a hint of fear. They don't have much time. I don't care what he'll do to me anymore. But I don't want anything to happen to them.

The nurse comes back in and hands me a clipboard. "I need

you to sign this AMA paperwork. I'm going to get you an Uber. Where do you want to go?"

I tell her my address. She types it in and looks at me. "That's two hours away."

I blink. Two hours away? Where am I?

"It's fine. I'll see if they'll do it. Walk with me."

She takes me through the hospital. I keep looking over my shoulder, expecting him to be there.

But he doesn't show up, not on the walk or while we wait for the Uber. While we wait, I ask to borrow her phone, and I call Kyle. He doesn't pick up, probably because of the strange number. I leave him a message.

My Uber driver looks annoyed. I open the door and then turn back to the nurse. I wonder if I should give her a hug or say something eloquent, but then I just turn and get into the car.

And then I leave.

We drive away from the hospital. He doesn't tell me to buckle up. We go through the town, passing a McDonalds and Walmart. We get to the open road and keep going.

I look over my shoulder, but no truck follows us.

It doesn't make me feel any different. This is a sick game. It was too easy. They're going to get me, and when they do, they'll make me pay worse than they ever have.

We drive and drive. There are some sighs from the driver, but I stay silent. He drives fast, like he can't wait to drop me off. After an hour, I start to recognize the scenery. Things get more and more familiar until we get to my old neighborhood.

I swallow.

We pull up to my house. It's dark. My car is still parked in the driveway. Kyle's is there, too, as well as a beat-up silver Honda I don't recognize.

I don't want to leave the car. As soon as I do, they'll pop out from the shadows, fling me over their shoulders, and do depraved things to me. The first real feeling hits me, and it's arousal.

That makes me snap up, and I get out. The driver doesn't let me say anything and speeds off. I stand there, looking after him.

Finally, when his lights are gone, I look at the house. My house. The lights are on.

It's surreal to be back here. Everything looks and feels the same. It's like I went on vacation, and now I'm back. Familiarity makes me smile slightly.

I walk toward the door, and my hospital gown brushes against my legs. Suddenly, I realize that things here might be the same, but I'm not.

I take a deep breath and try the door handle. It's locked. I pause before knocking. What would happen when I saw Kyle? Would I start crying? Would I beg for his forgiveness? Would he ever forgive me? The least he deserves, though, is to know I'm alive after all this time.

I knock.

It takes a bit, and I get strangely nervous on my own doorstep. But finally, it opens, and there he is behind the storm door, in his old white T-shirt and boxers.

I give an awkward wave.

He blinks. "Oh my god." He stares and stares and doesn't open the door.

"Uhhh, can I come in?" I try to joke as I reach for the door.

He steps back as I step in. The familiar scent of my home hits me, and out of nowhere, I tear up. I didn't realize I missed this smell so much.

"Jo! I—are you okay?"

My heart clenches. No, I'm not okay. Not at all okay. I look at Kyle and want to just fall into his arms and cry. I start to do that and catch movement behind him. I pause.

"Kyle?" The voice is feminine.

I freeze. Behind Kyle, a woman about our age wraps her sweater around her. She grimaces when she sees me. "Hey, Jo." She looks slightly familiar.

I take a step back. Kyle winces and rubs the back of his neck.

I look between the two of them. Finally, I ask, "What is she doing here?"

She tilts her nose up. "I'm his girlfriend, Jen."

The world crashes to a halt, and I focus on her face. Girlfriend? I try to swallow, but my mouth is too dry. Girlfriend? He was cheating on me. Anger flows through my system like a flame along dry wood.

Kyle clears his throat. "I thought...after your letter...that you were never coming back." He continues rubbing the back of his neck. "I didn't get rid of any of your stuff, you know, in case you still wanted it."

I look between the two of them. All I can do is clench my fists.

"Hey, are you okay?" Kyle motions at my gown.

I snort. The woman—Jen—glares at me. She's really pretty. Prettier than me. Suddenly, all my emotions leave again. It's like a wave of numbness sweeps everything back into the ocean.

"Can I get you—"

"No." I hold up a hand, trying to figure out what I'm going to do.

Kyle has a girlfriend. In my home. I can't stay here.

Jayden and Cole are coming for me. I know it. The longer I've been away, the more I've realized this isn't a game. I might actually be able to get away this time.

I look at Jen. "How much gas is in your car?"

"What?"

"How much gas? I'll trade your car for mine. Mine's fully paid off and newer."

Her mouth drops open. "You...want to take my car?"

"Please." I hate that Jayden and Cole have reduced me to pleading. But I want a car that they won't recognize. That the cops won't link to me. I look over my shoulder and out the storm door. I don't see any headlights approaching. Yet.

"What's going on, Jo?" Kyle asks.

I grit my teeth. What can I say to get them to work with me?

"I'm in trouble. Can I get some of my things? Please, let me borrow the car. You guys can have the house, too. I don't care."

They look at each other.

I growl. "I'm getting my stuff." I march past them and toward my room.

"Hey—I put your stuff in the pink room," Kyle says.

I stop, then slowly turn. The goddamn pink room. I go, and there are trash bags full of things. I rip them open, looking for clothes. When I find a pair of sweatpants and a shirt, I throw them on, then grab a trash bag and go to the front door.

"These your keys?" I take an unfamiliar pair off the wire boob hanger.

The woman doesn't say anything, so I look back at her.

She looks at Kyle. "She can't have my car."

"I don't care." I whirl on her. "I'm in trouble. Dangerous men are after me to try and take me again. *Kidnap* me again. You took my boyfriend and my life; the least you can do is allow me my freedom."

She sucks in a breath.

"What are you talking about, Jo? Are you okay? Why don't you take my car?" Kyle asks again. He looks at me like I'm crazy.

"I'm fine," I snap. "I need a car they don't recognize."

"I think you need help." Kyle pulls a phone out of his pocket.

"No!" I take a deep breath. "Fine. I'll take mine. Just don't call anyone. Please help me carry my things out. I'm in a hurry."

He still looks at me like I'm insane. I don't wait. I grab my keys and lug the bag out to my car. I realize I still don't have shoes on. Then I go in and grab the other two. I don't know or care what's inside. My pulse is pounding for me to hurry.

"Where's my wallet and my phone?" I ask Kyle.

He motions to the pink room. "I thought you had your phone with you." I snatch up my wallet from a dresser.

"Where are you going?"

"Better that you don't know." I stomp outside and let the door slam. I don't turn to take any last looks at the house. Clearly, this shit is over for me. Decided by the goddamned universe of shit herself.

I stalk to my car and slam the door. This is the life I thought about while at the cabin. Cried about. The life I fought so hard to get back to.

And now it seems so empty. I jam my keys in and let suburbia swallow me whole.

## 34

*Two Weeks Later*

"You need to eat." Cole drops a paper plate and sandwich on my computer keyboard.

"Not hungry."

He growls. "Then I'll force it down your goddamned throat. You're not helping matters."

I curl my lip at him but don't have the energy to do much else. I stare at the Google Earth images of Carissa's house. I keep thinking that if I look at it long enough, maybe they'll update the picture with her car in the driveway.

I don't deserve to eat. Or sleep. And I don't want to. Jo left us. She had a miscarriage. She miscarried my—our baby. I swallow. I made it so bad for her that she ran and hasn't looked back. The shirt she left at our cabin has stopped smelling like her.

I fling the sandwich across the hotel room.

"Fuck you, Jay." Cole gets in my face. "You're going to clean that shit up, then you're going to get your head out of your ass and get to work. We aren't going to get her back when you can't even function enough to eat or sleep."

I stare into his flashing eyes. He's taken care of me and the cabin as I tore everything to shit. He jumped in the car, no questions asked and rode with me to Texas, where we've been hunting Jo relentlessly, with no luck. Surveillance on Carissa's farmhouse is damn near impossible as the house is a mile back from the road with multiple ways in and out and a family full of shoot-first-ask-questions-later kinds of people.

I considered interrogating and killing every last one of them. The only thing that stopped me was knowing I'd have to look Jo in the eye and see the pain that murdering her best friend's family would cause. Which left us with very few options. In this day and age, it's hard to completely disappear, but it's like Jo dropped off the face of the map.

Cole's voice is soft, "This isn't the Jayden that got me through all those years."

That hits me like a bat to the stomach. I jerk my gaze up to him. He looks...lost.

Fuck. Now I'm hurting my best friend too. I scrub my hands down my face. I'm a piece of shit. I've never felt that about myself until now.

We sit in silence for a bit. Then I ask, "Do we have any more goddamned bread?"

# Mary Jo

### 35

*Six Months Later*

"THAT'S IT, BABY." THE MAN ABOVE ME RUBS HIS BEARD ON my cheek and neck as he thrusts his pelvis into me. He's hard behind his jeans. He has my wrists pinned above my head, and he's taking control, but something feels wrong. It's not right.

"Hey," I say, trying to swallow away the wrongness. "Want to spice it up a little?"

His pace stutters. "What?" He looks at me. His eyes are hazy and complacent.

I frown. "Spice it up?" He doesn't react. I pull at my arms. "Let go."

He does immediately. For some reason, that pisses me off more. I push him away, and he allows it. "You know what. I don't feel well."

He takes a tiny step back. "What?"

I can't explain what's wrong. I came onto him. I found him on Tinder and hounded him for a date. He said he was a Dom, and I was desperate to feel that. But I don't feel that spark, that fear, that electricity like I did with... them.

"I'm sorry. It's just not working." I push past him. He follows me out of the room.

"Wait. What happened?"

I snatch my keys from his kitchen table. Normally, I'd never go to a strange guy's house, but I decided to try and live a little.

I walk to his door, and he gives an exasperated sigh. "Fine. Have a nice night. Life. Whatever."

I don't even turn around. I slide into the junker that Carissa has been loaning me so my car and plates don't show up on the radar and drive off into the night. To avoid feelings of disappointment and longing, I dial Carissa. She answers on the first ring.

"Bitch, it's early as fuck. Was he a one-pump chump?"

I sigh, "No, just...I don't know. Not what I expected."

"What do you mean?" She gasps, "Did he have serial killer vibes? I'm coming over."

I laugh and look at the dark Texas countryside going by. No, he didn't. Is it sad that I'd probably have enjoyed it more if he did? I fill her in on the details.

"Well, okay. And hey, don't forget," she reminds, "You have that removal appointment this week. And don't bitch out this time. He'll never book me again if I keep promising him you'll show, and you never do."

I wince. "Fine, fine." I've been procrastinating on it. I'm not sure why; I just can't bring myself to go. The tattoo feels like...a part of me now.

I hang up with Carissa. When I do, the silence fills my mind, followed quickly by pain, emptiness, and homesickness. I tell myself it's for my old house with Kyle.

I jam on the radio and try to block out the memories. I still have nightmares. I feel guilty about Sage's death. Like maybe if I hadn't been so wrapped up in Jayden and Cole, I could have helped save her. The thought is an old friend at this point, with how much I've thought about it.

I roll into the farmhouse driveway and shut the car door

quietly. Despite the warm night, I shiver. Recently, I feel like someone has been watching me. I know it's PTSD, thinking someone is around every corner. But I can't shake the feeling.

The next morning, after I've made breakfast and cleaned the dishes, Rosemary comes up to me where I'm dusting the blinds. It's one of the most monotonous things to do and makes me want to shove the duster into my eye socket. But she pays me in cash and gives me a place to live. I've started back up on social media, using a different account, of course, but it takes time to build up the follower base that I left behind.

"This came for you, sweetie." She slides an envelope to me and moves into the kitchen.

It's a light blue envelope with the name 'Mary' printed on it and nothing else. My heart rate increases. I've been going by Mary here. I had never used it before Jayden and Cole. I always went by Jo, and it's easier to stick to a lie when it's a partial truth. But something about it feels wrong.

I take the envelope and tell myself it's nothing. Something from one of Rosemary's friends, maybe.

I open it and slide out a powder blue card with gold tree limbs and sparkles for leaves. There's a cabin in the background with gold wood. I swallow.

Inside the card is blank except for one word. I drop the card to the floor.

'Kitten'.

# COLE

## 36

I SIT BACK IN THE TRUCK, DRUMMING THE STEERING WHEEL. My dick gets hard thinking about the ways I'm going to punish her. I've been unbearably horny. Jacking off for the past six months just barely takes the edge off. I need to bury myself in her and make her scream. Make tears fall from those pretty eyes. Watch her bleed. Remind her she's ours, and we're the only ones that will ever satisfy her again. At the same time, I need to run my fingers through her hair and breathe her in. Listen to how her days have been without us. Listen to anything she wants to talk about. In the last six months, I realized that something happened between us. I...care about her. Something I never thought I'd be capable of feeling for anyone except Jayden. I rub my chest.

Just the thought makes me want to kill the fucker who had his hands all over her last night. I know he didn't get anywhere past a kiss. We beat that truth out of him. I grip the wheel so hard that my fingers turn white. I should have killed him anyway.

We're parked on the side of the road, about a mile from the house. Jayden lights up a cigarette, takes a puff, and offers it to me. I take it to get my leg to stop bouncing.

"Let's just go get her." He lights up another. "Waited long enough to play."

"It'll flush her out. Just wait."

I want to glare at him. These days have been the longest of my life. We slowed our pace for a few months and spent that time leaning into the suck of our pasts. Once I got out of that first two-week hell, I was hit with horrifying clarity that I wasn't ready to be a dad. Neither of us was, and we almost had been. Jayden spent a lot of time alone. I didn't ask what he was doing, but I suspected the same as me — soul searching.

But we never stopped looking for Jo. I looked every single day for her. Checking police reports, electric bills, traffic tickets, anything we could think of. And just a few days ago, our smart, opportunistic, *aggravating* thing made a fatal mistake.

One of her images popped up from a dating site of all things. The thought makes rage and laughter flit through my chest. The ballsy minx didn't use her real name, but she did use an old picture she'd posted on her real Facebook. I further confirmed it was her by searching for her fake name. A bunch of videos about her making food from various cultures flooded my feed. Seeing her face again soothed some deep part of me. From there, it wasn't hard for us to find her location, sitting right under our noses—so close to where we were that first two weeks.

It was almost like she wanted to be found.

Because she does.

She's going to pay. She's going to pay big time.

"I don't like this." I blow smoke out the window and flip my knife around my fingers.

"It'll work." Jayden leans back. "If there is one thing our kitten does best, it's run."

# Mary Jo

## 37

I SNEAK OUT THE BACK DOOR AS THE SUN GETS LOW IN THE sky. I swing my backpack with water and a change of clothes over my shoulder. The August heat instantly wraps me up. I've been thinking all day about running.

I feel bad for leaving Rosemary and Carissa, but I don't want to get them involved. I almost texted Carissa a few times today, but despite any of my warnings, she would have come roaring down here with guns, and I can't get her hurt.

I don't go to the barn to get my or Rosemary's car. They've probably staked it out. Two dangerous shadows lurking in the dark. The thought makes me shiver.

I jog to the road and go North, towards Carissa's house. It's all farmland here, framed with trees and scrub. I'll be able to hear and see any car that comes before they see me and dodge into the brush. It's stupid leaving before the sun sets fully, but I couldn't stay any longer. My blood felt like it was on fire, and the warning in my head told me to run before I couldn't anymore.

Adrenaline runs through my body, making my fingers numb. This what I've been waiting for all six months. That they'd find me. It feels like I'm playing an old game again.

A thrill runs through me. I take a deep breath. I feel alive. The sounds of my shoes on the gravel crunch crisply. The summer-baked grass smell is warm and delicious. I almost can't believe that any of this is real. Like maybe I've finally lost it, and I'm just seeing things now.

I can't keep a smile off my face. The smile is followed up by a delicious hit of fear. If they find me, they're going to fuck me up.

I jog until my lungs burn, and I slow. I've wondered all day how the fuck they found me. How long have they known I've been here? I think about them watching me, and it makes the hair on the back of my neck stand up.

An engine sounds down the road. I whirl around, scanning the empty road. My heart races. There's nothing there.

It's probably just a neighbor. I turn back around and keep going.

The engine gets louder. It sounds like they're flying. I mutter and get to the side of the road, peeking over my shoulder again. Headlights shine in the distance. Looks like a truck. I turn and duck behind a scrubby bush.

The noise gets louder, and I see the truck better.

My stomach drops, and dread courses through me. It can't be. The truck roars up to where I am and then slams on the brakes, stopping in a cloud of dust.

Maybe they haven't seen me. Maybe, maybe, maybe.

The driver's door opens, and a deep voice says, "I wouldn't stop if I were you."

My heart stops. His voice is gravelly and full of menace. "Cole's a little testy that you've gotten away this long."

I know I should be running. I feel like a bunny in the sight of a hawk. Maybe if I'm still enough, they won't see me. I'll be safe.

The passenger window rolls down, and Cole makes eye contact with me.

I draw in a breath so harshly that it makes my lungs hurt. I forgot how big he is. How easily he can hurt me.

I turn and sprint. I run faster than I've ever run in my life. I sprint down the side of the road, looking for a place to get over the fence. The road blurs past me. I feel like I'm flying over the ground, but I can't go fast enough.

Doors slam.

The hot wind whistles past my ears, and my shoes crunch. Oh god, I need to hide. I don't look to see if they're following, but I know they are. I can hear crunches and skitters and heavy, fast footsteps.

There's a downed part of wire fencing ahead. I hurtle towards it and jump over, flying through the field. I narrowly miss twisting my ankle in the uneven terrain. I don't even know where I'm going until something looms in the dimming light. A barn.

I run to it. The closer I get, the more I can see that it looks old and unused. The sliding doors sag open, and I slip inside.

Darkness blinds me for a moment. Then I see I've run into an abandoned barn with two stalls on both sides and an opening into a paddock at the opposite end. An old horse barn. I dart to the right and into one of the old stalls. Once behind the wall, I collapse on the bare rubber mats, digging in my bag for the knife I brought.

"Little one." The voice is deadly calm, coming from the arena. "I missed you. Come out and play."

The words hold promise and danger. They hang in the hot air. It makes lust settle deep in me.

What is wrong with me? I find my knife and grip it, trying to catch my breath in the stifling heat.

"Kitten."

I jump. The voice is close in the aisle I'm hiding in.

"Did you touch yourself without our permission? Make yourself come all over your desperate fingers?"

I swallow.

The other voice speaks up and is also close. "That's a broken rule, little one."

"Two broken rules..." The first voice speaks up, then abruptly stops.

I hold my breath. Everything goes unnaturally silent. I grip my knife harder, staring at the stall door.

"I told you not to run." Two massive forms slip inside the stall and roll the door shut with a screech and a bang.

I scream and jump to my feet, darting away from their reach to the back of the stall.

"Nowhere to go." Cole steps forward. He's dressed in black pants and a black T-shirt that's stretched across his muscled body. He has a grin on his handsome face. He looks like he wants to eat me alive.

I know what I'm about to say will make them angry and fuck me harder. It makes my heart race. "I played your stupid game. And I won. I beat you, Jayden." I swipe my knife out in front of me. "Just needed to come here to get that reminder?"

Jayden's gaze darkens to completely black. Cole throws his head back and laughs. "Just as cute as I remember." Cole eyes me and my knife. "You want to cut me again, lemon drop?"

"I want you to back off and go to hell." I feel more alive right now than I have in forever. My blood sings with electricity.

He just smiles and steps closer. "Do I make your panties wet?"

I glare at him.

"I think we should check." Jayden also walks closer, hunger all over his dark face.

My back is against the wall. They have me, and they know it. They look like lions playing with their food. I slash at Cole when he gets too close, but he just steps out of the way.

"There is no escape for you," Jayden growls and goosebumps prickle down my arms. He leans in, and his voice lowers. "We *will* hurt you. And you'll like it. But first," he cocks his head. I don't take my eyes off him. There's a battle in his eyes, and then his gaze softens, and pain fills it. He looks...vulnerable. His voice comes out low. "I'm sorry."

I freeze, and the barn is full of nothing but my heavy breathing.

"Me too, lemon drop."

My gaze darts between them. I lower my knife slightly and swallow.

Silence fills the barn. Jayden won't look at me, but Cole does, his gaze strong and soft. Sorry. They're sorry. For what? Kidnapping me? Making me watch them kill someone? The baby? I swallow.

My grip on the knife is almost painful. "I—I don't know what to say."

Jayden rubs the back of his neck and growls, "You don't have to say anything. Just accept that we're sorry, and we want to try again."

"I..."

Cole slips into an easy grin. "That doesn't change the fact you've broken rules."

I'm warned that the moment is over only by a glint in Jayden's eyes before he darts toward me. He moves so quickly that I hardly move before his huge body slams into me, and we both slam into the wall. His hand goes behind my head before it can crack off the wood. On reflex, I try to stab him, but my hand won't move. Cole is there, grinning. The game is on.

I scream. I scream loud and hard into Jayden's chest. He smells of musk and oil, and I catch spearmint too.

One of them groans.

I slam my head forward into Jayden's chest, putting all my pent-up energy into it. He just chuckles. The knife is stripped from my hand, and Jayden steps back. Before I can get away, he grabs my tank with his big hands and rips it down the middle. Cole's hands are around my waist, and he yanks my pants down.

He flicks the knife to my panties and bra, and suddenly, I'm naked in front of them while they're fully dressed.

Cole grabs my panties. "Yep. Soaked."

I feel exposed and turned on.

Jayden bends down and throws me over his shoulder.

I beat his back and ass. "Let me go. Put me down!" He doesn't. He carts me to the middle of the barn, where Cole throws an old tarp onto the dirt, and Jayden lays me down on my back. I scratch and claw, making contact with his skin, drawing beads of blood. His body feels warm and familiar. It's like my body remembers it and is drawn to him.

They flip me over, exposing my tattoo, and someone smacks my ass hard.

"Good girl. You didn't mess with it."

They flip me again. I glare up at them. Their eyes are molten with hunger. Jayden's nostrils flare and his pupils dilate.

"This is how it's going to go, kitten." Jayden reaches down to play with my breast. I smack him away, and he grins. "We're going to punish that beautiful body for defying us, for coming without permission, and for being so damn intoxicating, neither of us could let you go."

Cole adjusts himself.

"And if we punish you and you don't come, we'll let you go."

I look between both of them. They look serious.

I sneer. "You have to be turned on to come. Shouldn't be a problem." I turn and scramble away.

Hot, heavy hands clamp on my legs and yank me back, rustling the tarp and flipping me face up. It's Cole who has grabbed me. He runs his hand up my thigh while pinning my hip down with the other.

Despite the heat, my body gets goosebumps. He looks me in the eye as he goes higher. I look down my nose at him. He reaches my cunt and runs a finger along it, then holds it out in front of me. It glistens.

I glare. Both men wear smug looks. "Whatever you say, kitten."

"I hate you," I say with all the venom I can.

Cole winks at me. Jayden unzips his pants. "I've been thinking about those angry lips every day for the last six months." He pulls his dick out, and I'm reminded how big it is. "Suck while you ride him."

Cole groans and also pulls himself out. My body thrums at the sight of both of them, hard and glistening with precum.

I glare. "Part of the deal is you can't use your hands."

Jayden cocks an eyebrow.

"You can't use your hands to make me come. And once you both come, you don't get a chance to try again. When I win, you leave me alone. Forever. No hunting me down and making new stupid deals."

Jayden laughs but gives me a dark look. He looks at Cole, then shrugs. "Okay. Deal. Now suck."

Cole lays his big body down next to Jayden. I slowly throw my leg over his torso. He's warm and tense under me. Slowly, I move toward his pelvis. His hands twitch. Even slower, I reach down and grab his dick.

It's hot and jumps in my grasp. I drag his tip through my wetness. It feels good. It feels so good to be back around them. My body thrums with energy.

Cole clenches his jaw while looking at me. I cock an eyebrow and insert just the head inside of me. He groans but holds himself still, tendons in his neck standing out. I don't lower any further.

I open my mouth for Jayden. Slowly, ever so slowly, I lick from his base to his tip. His scent fills my senses, and I slowly hollow my mouth and suck the tip.

Jayden groans. I feel a tremor run through Cole. "Little one," he grits.

I dig my nails into him, bouncing the tiniest bit on him, and he groans. I tease them both like that, building their anticipation and giving them a little, but not enough.

"Kitten." Jayden grabs my jaw.

I pull away from him and snap. "No hands."

He releases me with a smirk. "You said to make you *come*."

"She did, didn't she." Cole grabs my hips and slams into me.

I gasp. He feels huge, and the stretch is slightly painful.

"I don't care if it hurts," Cole growls. "You'll take it like a good girl. This pussy is already weeping for me." He slams into me repeatedly. I'm so wet that he slides in with little resistance. I dig my fingernails into his chest.

With one hand, I grab Jayden again and suck him all the way down my throat. I work him hard and fast, licking and sucking, and pulling him down.

He throws his head back, baring his muscled neck. I know I have him close when he swallows, his Adam's apple bobbing. I continue hard and fast with the rhythm I had.

He rips out of my mouth. I catch my breath, but Cole slams into me hard enough to take my breath right back. "Are you trying to get him to come so soon, little one?" He pounds in and shifts so that he's hitting my G spot over and over.

I groan, then collect myself enough to blow him a sarcastic kiss. "Never, pretty boy."

Cole's eyes flare, and quicker than I can blink, he's flipped me over and is hovering over me. "Mouth, Jay."

Cole pulls out, and immediately a hot mouth covers my clit and sucks hard.

My body bucks in surprise and pleasure. Fuck. I squirm to get away. Large hands with an iron grip clasp my thighs and keep me still. Cole reaches into his pocket and flips something out. A knife.

"Six months of running. Tinder? You just don't remember who you belong to, do you?"

Jayden gives a hard suck, and pleasure shoots through me again.

"I'm not an object to be possessed," I growl.

Cole looks at me, blue eyes impassive. He looks the same as I remember from before, but maybe slightly older. "No. You're a woman with heart, mind, and body. We want to worship every last piece of every last part of you. Whether you give it willingly or not. But I'm going to guess it's willingly."

Jayden continues to lick and suck, and pleasure fills me. I grab his hair and dig my fingers into his scalp.

Cole skims the edge of the knife on his finger, watching my face. "I'm going to remind you what your body accepts, but your mind doesn't."

He grabs my right hand and pries it from Jayden's scalp. He pins it to his knee with one hand, and the other brings the tip of the knife to my forearm.

I freeze. Jayden continued to lick me while grabbing a bottle of something out of his cargo pants. Antiseptic.

Shit. I start to struggle, but Jayden has my hips pinned, and Cole presses the tip of the blade close enough that my movement causes a burst of pain.

"If you want this to look sloppy, keep fighting. But I would suggest you lie still." Cole waits for a beat to see how I'm going to react.

I breathe heavily, staring at the knife indenting into my skin. Then I look at him. "What are you doing, you crazy bastard?"

"Reminding your mind who you belong to." He takes the hand that was pinning my arm and pops open the antiseptic. I watch as he sprays it on my arm and the knife that's still dug into me. It burns.

Panic fills me. "What are you *doing*?" I start to struggle.

Jayden nips the inside of my thigh in a warning. "It's a small mark, kitten. Lay still. We won't let anything bad happen."

Cole looks into my eyes. His pupils are blown. "We have yours on us."

"What?" My heart is still pounding.

Cole raises his right arm. On his tanned skin, there's a white, raised 'J.' Oh shit. He scarred himself.

"J for Jo. Jayden has M for Mary."

I look at Jayden. His dark eyes meet mine right above my pelvis. His gaze is filled with lust. "He'll make it easy, kitten. Lay down." He lowers his head and closes his mouth on me again.

Adrenaline courses through me. Cole doesn't wait. He cuts into my arm, and I buck up in a burst of pain. He keeps me still with his other hand.

"Easy, little one." He murmurs but doesn't stop. Pain lights up down my arm, and I can't take my eyes away. Blood beads up under the blade. It hurts like a bitch, but I can tell he isn't cutting deep.

"Beautiful skin," he mutters, "Like butter."

I don't realize that Jayden has been sucking my clit until he gives a particularly hard pull, and my hips buck up. He grumbles, and the noise vibrates against me. The adrenaline amplifies the sensation, making sparks fly in my vision. I grit my teeth and groan. The pain, mixed with the fear, makes my head fuzzy, and pleasure mixes in.

And I let it happen.

Wave after wave of pleasure and pain fills me. I scrunch my eyes closed. Tension builds. Suddenly, Jayden moves his jaw while sucking, and pleasure explodes. I come, lights shooting behind my eyes in a blinding explosion. It goes on and on, and Jayden continues to pull and suck. I cry out and arch my back.

The pleasure and pain swirl in the fog. Slowly, it starts to clear, and I realize that Cole has put the knife away and wrapped my arm in a white bandage.

Jayden looks up at me with an evil smile on his face. He licks his lips. "Looks like you lost, kitten."

I jerk up.

"No, no, lay back down. Cole needs that mouth after playing with his knives. And I need this beautiful, hot cunt. It's been too long."

They both move quickly, bodies tense. Jayden kneels between my legs and fills me in one stroke. I gasp, pleasure shooting through me again. Cole gently grabs my chin and faces me to him. I move up on my elbows. He puts my lips to the tip of his cock. His voice is gravelly, and he sounds out of control. "Make it hurt, baby."

I do. I take him into my mouth and rake my teeth along him. He throws his head back and groans. I suck him fervently, grabbing his dick at the base and squeezing, nicking him with my nails. He thrusts down my throat as Jayden continues to pound into me. It's rough and brutal, both men chasing their own rhythm and force. But it doesn't keep me from coming again, tightening on Jayden's dick as I cry out around Cole's.

"Fuck." Cole's movement stutters, and he comes hard down my throat. Jayden grunts, stiffens, and yanks out of me, shooting on my tits and stomach. Cole pulls out, and I suck in a deep breath.

We all catch our breath, the only sound in the muggy, dim light. Slowly, I realize that I'm still on the dirty tarp in the old barn with the two men who hunted me down.

Cole leans down and kisses me on the forehead. Jayden tucks himself away and scoops me into his arms. My right arm brushes him, and I make a startled noise of pain.

"Let's go get you cleaned up, kitten."

My arms and legs are limp with happy exhaustion. I close my eyes against the rocking of our bodies. I can tell when we leave the barn when the night air hits me with a warm puff and the smell of hay. Crickets chirp, and the men's footsteps crunch in the dirt.

Jayden smells warm and familiar. We walk for a while until I hear his boots hit the gravel road. I stir.

Jayden growls, "We're taking you back, kitten. Did you really think we wouldn't come unprepared? If you fight me, we'll drug you."

I wasn't going to fight them. Not for real anyway. But he doesn't have to know that.

They carry me to Jayden's truck. I recognize it with a lurch of my stomach. It's the one he dragged Sage out of to kill her.

They throw me in the back. Cole slides in beside me as usual. He leans over, straps me in, then kisses my forehead. "Welcome back, little one. You're fucked now."

Jayden winks at me in the mirror, and we drive off into the darkness.

*A Note From Alina*

If you've made it this far, you truly are some dirty, nasty hoes (or you can't DNF a book...which fair cause neither can I). I would love to get to know you better! You can join my Facebook group Alina May's Book Babes.

You can also find me on my website at alina-may-books.squarespace.com

An extra thank you to my editor, Allie from Falcon Faerie Fiction. We started off as strangers and we ended as friends. Thanks for everything, babe!

Made in United States
North Haven, CT
24 July 2024

55386398R10154